HOUND DOG
BLUES

W.C. MAYBORN

DEDICATION

This book is for my three fantastic kids and my amazing wife.

ACKNOWLEDGEMENT

This book would not be possible with the support of friends and family who helped me write this novella. A large thank you is extended to the following people: Max Bryan, Brian Fisher, Katie Fuerst, Matt Jacobs, Don Mayborn, Cheryl Mayborn, Tina Mayborn, Chris McGuffey, Jackson McGuffey, Mike Shaub, Chris Tomescu, Jim Wallace and Brian White.

Chapter 1- City Heat

Chicago never does well in the heat, and the summer of 2012 was boiling. The locals' blood is too thick from the harsh winters, so when the temperatures hit the boiling point, tempers rise and people do things they regret. For Maurice "Hound Dog" Jackson the weather suited him fine since he grew up south of the Mason Dixon Line.

He had his fourth floor apartment windows open and the sounds of the street were wafting through his fourth floor apartment along with a pungent mix of diesel and greasy food. The dominant fixture of the apartment was Hound Dog's "shrine", as he called it, containing all of his coveted Blues records. The rest of his little apartment was modestly decorated with Blues posters of all the greats, and the simple furnishings of a bed and dresser.

Hound Dog was singing to himself, working on one of his melancholy inducing Blues songs. He strummed a few bars and told his wolf, Sasha, "I think I'm going to call this one, 'Howling Lonely'".

Been lonely so long I don't know what to do,
Ever since she left me I've been so blue,
My hearts been aching for so long,
You know I've been done wrong.

When I wake up in the morning,
My hurting heart couldn't even sing,
It is barely ticking over like an old Dodge,
I feel like a lonely wolf.

"I put that last part in there for you, Sasha."

But naturally there was no response from the wolf. Being the lonely man that he was, Hound Dog often talked to his pet wolf, and he often talked to himself aloud. Besides, there was no one else around to complain that he shouldn't talk to Sasha.

Hound Dog was feeling frustrated because he couldn't put the final words together, so he decided to strum on his old Martin six string and let his mind relax. The words would come in due time, but it would be nice to have them for tomorrow's recording session at Tri-City Records. Most of the old gang would be there; it was going to be great. Dan "the Man" Church was going to be on bass, Jimmy "Longhorn" Wallace and Hound Dog on the electric guitars, and Max "Volume" Bryan on the drums.

He was thinking out loud for the benefit of Sasha to hear, "Al said he couldn't find someone for the street organ." The group needed some deep, rich support that comes from the organ.

Matt "Fingers" Jacobs had been his organist for seven years, but a disagreement over French fries had divided their friendship. Fingers had insisted on calling French fries, "Freedom fries", even though it was 2012 and everyone in the Western Hemisphere had reverted back to calling them French fries. But Fingers was a stickler and got angry a few months ago when they were eating at Ruth's Rib Shack.

"Sasha, can you believe that guy, Fingers? He left the band over a silly thing like what to call French fries. And now we're left in a lurch because we can't find a replacement. The nerve of some people!"

At that moment, Hound Dog thought back to some of his own ridiculous arguments he had waged with people. Some of the disagreements he couldn't even remember what they were arguing over, but he distinctly remembered the people and the broken relationships. "Maybe I should give Fingers a phone call. What have I got to lose?"

Hound Dog picked up his phone and started dialing the old familiar number for Fingers' house.

Fingers answered the phone, "What do you want Hound Dog?"

"How did you know it was me?" asked Hound Dog.

"What decade are you in, man? It's called 'call waiting'; I can see your name displayed on the phone when it rings. You should be happy I answered when I saw your name…"

"Well, I'll cut to the chase, Fingers; we need a street organ player for a recording session tomorrow at Tri-City Records. Can you come tomorrow morning at nine?"

"You know as well as I do, Tri-City Records doesn't have any money to pay the band. What are they going to do, buy us some donuts and hope the electricity stays on long enough to record an album?"

"So I guess your schedule is too busy to come and play some Blues tomorrow." There was silence on the other end of the phone. Hound Dog knew that the Blues had a grip on Fingers that was more satisfying than cash in his pockets.

"Okay, I'm in," conceded Fingers.

Hound Dog smiled, "And look, I will buy you some Freedom fries for lunch tomorrow." "Freedom fries? Hound Dog it's 2012."

Hound Dog couldn't believe Fingers had flip-flopped on the French fry name! Caught off guard, "Well… um… I'll see you in the basement recording studio at nine, sharp."

"Gotcha; see you tomorrow," said Fingers, "And thanks for giving me a call."

"My pleasure," replied Hound Dog, "Have a good night."

As Hound Dog hung up the phone and thought to himself, *Playing the Blues is a heck of way to earn a living.*

It is part of the conundrum that faces every Blues player. The successful ones sell albums like hotcakes, go on big, fancy tours with Rock stars, and start living a life of the rich and famous. Their lives get complicated and they lose all their potential writing material. Can you expect them to write songs that denigrates their own wealth? Hound Dog imagined himself introducing his song to an audience: "Don't you just hate those luxury car Blues?"

When I woke up this morning, my Mercedes was in the shop,
I had to drive the Rolls-Royce that I reserve for Sunday drives,
Oh, I couldn't bear the sight, driving my Silver Ghost on a rainy day,
I had to have the butler buff out all the spots and give it a second wash.

"Or maybe something like this"

I got the stock market Blues, can't stand it no more,
The NASDAQ was down at lunch time, and the DOW was looking bleak,
Before I could unload my tech stocks, I got hit by the Fed low'rin the rate,
What's a man to do when he has the stock market Blues?

Hound Dog didn't have to worry about those problems; he had plenty of Blues material and had enough trouble making his rent every month. He played every venue that would take him and had lots of experience in not getting paid in full. Such as the time he played at a fraternity party when the "House Rocking" Blues was popular with the college kids. From that experience he always makes sure that the fraternity treasurer pays him upfront, *before* they buy the beer.

Another time he got ripped off by some loser in St. Louis and had to sing the Blues inside a truck stop just to earn enough gas money to get back to Chicago. It was on that trip that a truck driver placed Sasha inside his guitar case as a tip, and said, "Take care of her and she will be more loyal than your best friend."

Hound Dog at the time didn't know that the little black fur ball sitting at his feet was a wolf pup; he thought she was just an ordinary dog. But she has grown exponentially and has nearly eaten him out of house and home. Indeed Sasha has grown to be Hound Dog's most loyal friend, and she goes on every road trip with him. Plus, she is much more effective than any car security system that whistles and beeps when thunder claps. And with roughly 1,200 pounds per square inch of force in those front canines she could easily crush a car thief's bones into kibbles and bits. Usually her barking and barred teeth were deterrent enough to keep their grubby little hands off of Hound Dog's beloved Lincoln Mark III.

As the heat of the day subsided Hound Dog knew that tomorrow held the promise of a new album. It was going to be a beautiful day.

Chapter 2- Progress Report

It was much later than the boss expected to hear back from the crew, but he was relieved to get the call at 3 am. He answered, "Harry's Hamburger House, can I take your order?"

"Boss, we didn't find the stash, but we got more than enough cash to cover it."

"I'm sorry; you must have the wrong number."

Each side ended the call without salutations.

Chapter 3- Recording Gone Wrong

Hound Dog and Sasha arrived early at Tri-City Records on West Third St. and proceeded down to the basement recording studio. The recording studio would remain cool for a good part of the morning since it was in the basement. Plus, all of the mattresses used for sound proofing insulated the room as well. The band would be able to get a good three hours in, break for lunch, and call it a day. Max and Dan had other jobs to attend to in the afternoon, so finishing early would help them out.

As Hound Dog strode by all the pictures of the great Blues musicians and R&B recording artists he paid his respects to his Blues mentor—Mike "Saw Tooth" Prather. Not much to look at, but he could sing the Blues with the best of them. Saw Tooth was a huge signing back in the day for Tri-City Records and helped put them on the map. Hound Dog's Blues career has been quite the contrary, Tri-City weren't impressed with Hound Dog's abilities and it took them a couple of years before they signed him to a contract. Without Saw Tooth's coaching and prodding Hound Dog's playing and singing abilities wouldn't have matured in the least.

From the looks of the place, Tri-City Records had seen better days. The music company occupied three floors above ground for offices, record production and storage. Below ground used to be the most state of the art recording studio in Chicago, but that was back before eight tracks, tapes, CDs, and eventually digital media became popular. The nails in the coffin have been adding up ever since Al Gore invented the

Internet; poor Tri-City records became a speed bump on the information super-highway.

It didn't help that Al Porter, the owner of Tri-City Records, was distrustful of "highfalutin" technology and resisted anything digital. He said he was a traditionalist, but truth be told he really didn't have the capital to overhaul his operations. Al argued that he knew how to cut the best record albums anywhere in the mid-west, and to complete his illogical reasoning he argued, "Why would anyone want tapes or CDs?" So the once proud Tri-City Records was now hobbling on its last legs and Hound Dog was surprised it was still alive and kicking. Yet, through it all Hound Dog was loyal to his contract with Al, and Al had always treated him well, so he stuck with Tri-City. The real break-through came when Hound Dog worked out a deal with Al that allowed Hound Dog to transfer his music from the record albums into mp3s and sold on the Internet.

As Hound Dog entered the basement studio he was happy, almost giddy to cut another album. "Sasha, you lay down in your spot in the control room," said Hound Dog to his loyal wolf. Sasha knew her spot out of the way, but still close enough to her master. Wolves are intensely social animals.

Inside the recording room, Jimmy "Longhorn" Wallace was tuning up and getting his fingers warmed up. Longhorn came from a long tradition of Texas guitarists, and he was Hound Dog's favorite. Longhorn couldn't sing, not even a gasp, but he could play a mean guitar like nobody's business; the type of guitar playing that makes a person start swaying and clapping along. Hound Dog would often indulge Longhorn and let him play extended solos, and the crowds usually ended on their feet by the end of the sweet, yet grinding style. Longhorn was focused on getting ready, so Hound Dog let him have the time to himself. They were good enough friends that a nod and a smile were enough to acknowledge they were going to rock out today.

Dan "the Man" Church kicked the door and swung his bass guitar case through. "Whoa! Good to see you Hound Dog! Are you ready to cut this album?!" Dan was his usual enthusiastic self, and it was a real plus to have his excitement around the studio.

Dan "the Man" Church was a south side Chicago native, and he played the bass better than anyone around. He was also a vacuum tube aficionado, and you can tell he likes the rich, deep sound. Dan carried extra vacuum tubes for his amp and was always on the lookout for old ones here and there in old TV sets and radios.

"Good to see you, Dan. How's the family?" asked Hound Dog.

"They're doing well; the little one is taller than me now. They sure do grow up quickly."

Around that time, Max "Volume" Bryan came striding through the door. His tall frame barely missed the top of the door. His sticks were in hand, and he was all ready to go. He must have come in early to set up his drum kit. Max had all the drums just where he likes them; for such a tall guy, he keeps his drums low to the ground so he can beat down on them. You don't get a nickname like "Volume" for nothing, because when he is really rocking and banging the drums he gets extremely loud; we're talking Spinal Tap "11" loud. To match his unrivaled intensity was his flawless speed and rhythm. Hound Dog counted himself fortunate to have such a great drummer that could have played for some of the top rock bands in Chicago, but Max "Volume" chose to play with Hound Dog and the gang.

"Hey Max, are you ready to keep us on time?" asked Hound Dog knowing full well that Volume was born with a metronome in his brain.

Not much for words this early in the morning, Volume answered with a quick, "Sure."

"It looks like we are just waiting on Fingers and "Lightning" Watkins to show up."

Jeff "Lightning" Watkins was the recording specialist groomed by Al Porter to record and cut the records. He got the name "Lightning" from being faster than the speed of sound in the control room. He could do wonders with the whole analog set up. It was a lost art, but he was the maestro behind the window. Lightning also played the role of the perfectionist that every recording studio needs to keep the ship aright; he wasn't afraid to step on somebody's toes to make sure things were done right. He lived by the words, "Anything worth doing; is worth doing right." What self-respecting musician could argue with that creed; music was more than their livelihood it was their passion.

Hound Dog knew this group loved to make music that could stir peoples' feet and shake their hearts to the core. It was Chicago Blues—gritty and raw, fast and furious, soulful and rich. Chicago Blues has a driving, upbeat combination of raw sound, blaring guitar, with support from the street organ and bass, with the drums coming along to keep a steady beat in the background. Hound Dog couldn't imagine playing anything else.

Hound Dog saw his role as lead vocalist and lead guitar as an opportunity to lead a symphony of Blues. It was a thing of beauty—

putting all the pieces together and letting them all balance each other. Hound Dog's vocals were there to bring the emotion and heart ache. That's one of the large areas where Saw Tooth helped Hound Dog develop, but the nickname was already attached. Deep, hearty, strained songs came streaming from his mouth. Details of a life without love are what Hound Dog sang about. People in the audience usually don't know what to do when they hear him singing alongside a vibrant, rocking band. Should they dance or cry?

Then Fingers came through the door. He looked disheveled and a little out of sorts. "You okay, Fingers?" asked Dan "the Man".

"Yeah, I'm alright; just had an argument with the little lady at home." Everyone in the band knew that Finger's wife was not of petite proportions, but they were all prudent not to mention it.

"Well, you ready to play some Blues? You can use those painful emotions to fuel your playing," offered Hound Dog.

"Thanks, but I don't need a motivational speaker. Let's get recording," Fingers fired back sharply.

During that interchange, Lightning had slipped into the control room and was getting all the recording equipment squared away. He spoke over the intercom, "Sorry I'm late Hound Dog. I was upstairs working on some bills." Lightning practically ran Tri-City Records these days. He did everything to keep the sinking ship afloat a little longer; which can be hard for a perfectionist. But recording great Blues was his passion.

Hound Dog could feel his heartbeat starting to race, "Alright guys, you ready to make some Blues history? Let's start out with something nice and tight—'Route 66 Runaway'. Fingers will take the lead, and then we'll all come rocking right in behind him." Hound Dog led the count, "One-two-three-four!"

Then it was pure Blues ecstasy. Fingers was inspired by the morning argument with his wife; he hit the keys and the organ gave a vibe of melancholy that was both depressing and vengeful. Hound Dog knew it was going to be a good set and gave a nod to Longhorn. Longhorn and Hound Dog came right along to whip up some good guitar riffs. And then came time for the vocals:

> *Baby, please don't you run away from me,*
> *You know I love you too much, to see you go,*
> *I said! Baby, please don't you run away from me,*
> *Because Route 66, leads away from home.*

Fingers and Longhorn collaborated on an interlude between verses, and were really jamming. And then Hound Dog started into the next verse:

> *Baby, please don't do me wrong,*

It was at this point that Hound Dog noticed the mattresses behind Max started shaking. Hound Dog thought to himself, *We must have hit some crazy harmonic vibration to get the mattress springs jumping.* And he continued to sing:

> *I don't want you to run...*

And Hound Dog stopped singing mid-verse when a few mattresses burst off the wall behind Max Volume. Out of the wall came three policemen shouting, "Get your stinking hands in the air!" The music ended abruptly like a bad car crash, a cacophony worse than a junior high band warming up.

"What the heck-a-schmack? You can't burst into our recording studio!" yelled Hound Dog.

"Some criminals robbed the Third National Bank's last night by digging a tunnel right into the vault. And you guys are our prime suspects!" yelled the lead policeman.

Hound Dog was getting hot under the collar, and his mood tie started to change to red. "That's nonsense; can't you see we're playing the Blues. How do you know we are the ones who robbed the bank?"

"Shut-up, freak! We're the ones asking the questions! Four million dollars was stolen last night and I'll take you in right now, scum-bag!" retorted the lead officer.

Hound Dog was steaming mad that his recording session had been interrupted and yelled back at the police, "Go climb back into your rat hole and get out of here!"

The police officer in charge didn't like Hound Dog's attitude and threatened him with a drawn pepper mace spray can, "I'll spray this right down your lousy throat if you don't shut up!"

Hound Dog hates things pointed in his face, and he flew off the handle before any of the group members could hold him back. With a swift flick of his wrist he slapped the pepper mace out of the policeman's hand, unplugged the guitar from its electrical connection, and slammed the officer in the forehead with the guitar—knocking him out cold. As another officer came with a baton, Hound Dog swung the point of the guitar into his sternum and dispatched his baton with a down swing. Next, he kicked him in the chest and sent him into the third officer who was going for his sidearm. Before the two officers could recollect themselves, Hound Dog jumped over to them and knocked their heads together. They were out of commission, out cold on the floor.

This is when Hound Dog realized he was in big trouble.

Chapter 4- Run For the Hills

"You've got to get out of here Hound Dog," yelled Lightning over the studio intercom, "the cops will be coming after you!"

Hound Dog was in a panic, he ran over to his guitar case, placed in his beloved American Special Fender Stratocaster, and told the band, "Hang tight guys, we will get this thing recorded someday!"

The band looked glum at the prospect of putting off recording, but they knew that Hound Dog was in trouble with the law and needed to run.

Making his way out he called to Sasha, "Let's go girl!" and Sasha was up and ready to follow. Fortunately she hadn't heard the excitement coming from the recording studio or she might have gone crazy and attacked the police.

Hound Dog and Sasha were quickly up the basement stairs and out to street level. Hound Dog's heart was pounding in his head like a sledgehammer. He expected to see more cops rushing around, but reasoned that the three officers below hadn't the chance to call for back-up. Hound Dog decided to not make a scene by running on the street, but walked briskly back to his apartment a couple blocks away. He looked over his back, and thought he was going to make a run for it when a police car drove by. Talking in a muffled voice to Sasha, "I guess they don't know who their looking for, yet. I've probably got 30 minutes to make a run for the hills."

On the way home Sasha had to relieve herself by a tree and this gave Hound Dog time to make a mental checklist of the necessary steps to go underground for a good while before this thing could blow over.

Because of the delay with Sasha, Hound Dog even debated whether he would be able to take Sasha with him. On one hand he couldn't leave her, she was a great companion, and no one would want a 180 pound wolf to take care of, anyway. But then what kind of give-away would it be to have a giant black wolf traveling around with him. Everybody knows I go everywhere with her. Maybe he could dye her coat white! He was getting irrational.

Hound Dog approached the apartment building that looks like the picture on Led Zeppelin's *Houses of the Holy* album. Once he was inside the apartment's main doorway he and Sasha bound up the stairs as quickly as they could go. He was in a hurry to get out of Chicago before the cops could figure out who knocked out three cops in the basement of Tri-City Records.

He threw his suitcase on the bed and loaded it up with clothing, and reached under the dresser to grab a large roll of cash that was hidden underneath. Talking to himself, "Break glass in case of emergency. I think this situation qualifies." Hound Dog's heart was still pounding as the repercussions of his actions this morning were coming over him. He couldn't believe he fought off three cops and thought to himself, *That's gotta' add up to some serious prison time.*

"Sasha, we're going on a road trip." The wolf knew the suitcase cue from countless trips through the years and readied herself by the door.

"It's going to be fun, girl. The open road, truck stops, rest stops, greasy food. We will both gain 20 pounds by the end of the month. It is going to be part of our disguise," said Hound Dog as he tried to bring a little levity to the situation.

Hound Dog made sure to grab his prized possessions that were all held in an old cigar box—random items from his past such as a favorite pocket knife, his passport, his dad's fake Rolex wristwatch, a favorite baseball card, and his guitar pick collection. He would have to leave the "shrine" in place. There was no time to move over four hundred records; all those records would fill up the trunk.

The man and his wolf were out their apartment door and heading downstairs much faster than he thought it would take him. "We're making good time, Sasha. Let's go to the car and get going."

Hound Dog scoped out the street level before opening the door. No sign of the police on the street. The wolf could sense that her master was nervous and she responded by being more alert and ready for action. They made their way to Hound Dog's other most prized possession: a 1971 Lincoln Mark III—all black and ready to roll. Too bad he was going to have to trade it in for something else.

Chapter 5- The Detectives

A few hours later two police detectives were sitting in Al Porter's office at Tri-City Records. The furnishings were utilitarian and well-used as if they were all purchased from a postal auction. The detectives were serious and to the point, "Mr. Porter, I'm Detective Fortnight, and this is my partner, Detective Cole from the 9th Precinct. We're going to need to ask you a few questions about the robbery of the 3rd National Bank of Chicago. Is that alright with you?"

"Sure, I'd be happy to help," answered Al.

"Were you aware that a tunnel was being dug from your basement recording studio into the bank's vault?" asked Fortnight.

"No, I wasn't. If I was, I surely would have reported it," responded Al.

Fortnight kept firing away with the questions, "Have you noticed any suspicious activity around here?"

"No," Al answered.

"What are your normal business hours?" asked Fortnight.

"We are open nine to five, five days a week," responded Al.

Cole interjected, "Can we see a list of people that have had access to the recording studio in the past month?"

"Why of course, the list is on the chalkboard. That's where we keep track of who is recording or rehearsing their sets, and what days and when," answered Al.

Cole took a picture of the list with his smart phone, while his partner kept asking questions. He emailed the photo to a colleague at the precinct with the subject line, "3rd National Bank Heist-Key Suspects" and rejoined the conversation.

"To your knowledge do any of these recording artists have any large debts, or troubles with finances?" asked Fortnight.

"You got to be kidding me; they're Blues musicians. They are all down on their luck and earn their living singing about it," answered Al.

The detectives were not amused, but they played along with Al. They each gave a half-hearted chuckle to keep the conversation rolling. Al was visibly nervous, but kept volunteering information, "Take Hound Dog for instance, he can sing with the best of them, but he hasn't sold a record in long time. In the dog-eat-dog world of the music industry he is like a Chihuahua."

"Have you heard any odd noises coming from the basement? For example, any drilling noises, hammering, or loud unusual sounds coming from the basement?" asked Cole.

Al responded, "Can't say that I have; the room is completely sound-proofed by the mattresses, so that must have muffled the noise coming from the tunnel construction."

"How many people have access to Tri-City Records after hours?" asked Fortnight.

"Oh, a number of artists are provided a key so they can move their instruments in and out of the recording studio when they need them for their evening gigs or setting up for a morning rehearsal or recording," responded Al.

"Has anyone been spending inordinate amounts of time rehearsing or hanging out in the basement studio?" asked Cole.

Peering over the shoulders of the detectives Al took a glance, "From the looks of the black board, it looks like Hound Dog has been down there a lot lately."

The detectives made notes in their smart phones and kept asking Al questions.

Unfortunately, most of the names on the chalk board weren't the performers' real, legal names, so the detectives would have to get all of the aliases worked out.

"Do you know of any individuals under contract with Tri-City Records with a criminal record?" asked Cole.

Al folded his hands while he answered, "We are not in the habit of asking that when they sign a contract, but plenty of them sing about doing hard time in the penitentiary. Some of them could be just making it up though. You know what I mean: prison songs about being on chain gangs or breaking boulders."

"Thanks for your time, Mr. Porter. We're going to need some help figuring out the identities of the artists, could you assist us in supplying their personal information? For example we need to see their social security numbers, addresses, phone numbers; that sort of thing."

Al Porter stood up and said, "That shouldn't be a problem. We keep their files over here." Al and the detectives walked over to the lone filing cabinet in the office and pulled open the top drawer, "Which artists would you like to know more about?"

Chapter 6- New Wheels

Slick's Used Car Palace and Garage was not your ordinary, run-of-the-mill used car lot. It had a full selection of foreign and domestic luxury cars and a full service garage. Hound Dog knew he could get a solid trade in on his prized 5,000 pound lead sled. Some may consider such a heavy car environmentally uncouth, but one has to admit the Mark III has style. It was more than a car to Hound Dog; it was his chariot. Not to mention it could fit all of the band's guitars and amps in the trunk without any problems.

Hound Dog eased the car into a parking spot and finished the Blues song in the eight track player. He needed all the encouragement he could get and he didn't like ending a song in the middle. Especially when you have the volume cranked up. The song, "Love Gone Sour" by Nellie Best was on its last verse:

> *Why you say you love me,*
> *But you never buy me nothing nice,*
> *Why you say you love me,*
> *But you're always walking out the door.*

Hound Dog sat there soaking up the guitar playing, and he closed his eyes to enjoy the Blues as if it was washing over him.

Slick himself came out to meet Hound Dog. Sasha's eyes narrowed on him as he quickly approached the car; Sasha might have smelled Slick's cat, Marshmallow, or it could have been Slick's cheap Chinatown cologne, Yolo by Raelf Bauren. Hound Dog tried to calm Sasha, "It's okay, girl. He's a friend." It's not that Slick was a bad guy; he just had a bad nickname. He got it back in his car racing days when he raced with slick tires. Next thing he knew he had a nickname with a potentially derogatory meaning. But it beat Slick's legal name, Alfred Mannheimster, by a long stretch. Try surviving middle school with a name that sounds like Man-Hamster.

"Good to see you, Slick," said Hound Dog, putting out his hand to shake Slick's hand.

"You need some work done on the Mark III; or you looking to trade up to something nicer?" said Slick the constant salesman.

"You know I really need something faster, and that gets better gas mileage; you know with $4 gasoline this car is killing me at the pump."

"Tell me about it; diesel is even more expensive," said Slick as he pointed over to his huge monster truck parked over in the corner of the lot. It was a huge all black Ford F-350 dually diesel with big mudding tires and a huge lift.

"Wow, I like those special smoke stacks coming out of the bed," said Hound Dog.

"You know it's for sale." In fact everything on the lot was for sale. You had to watch your belongings because Slick would sell anything quicker than greased lightning.

"Don't you find the truck a little… over the top?" said Hound Dog.

"How do you figure?" snapped back Slick.

"Oh, never mind," knowing that time was of the essence Hound Dog didn't want to get bogged down in the non-utilitarian nature of a huge monster truck. Not to say that massive amounts of torque and huge tires weren't cool and all, but it's just not practical for a guy that parks it in the middle of South Chicago.

"You know Hound Dog; you mentioned you are looking for something fast. Today's your lucky day, because I've got a real beauty of a cop car over here," said Slick, not wanting to lose the momentum on a potential sale.

"Sure, I'll take a look at it," said Hound Dog, thinking that if he was going to be pursued by the cops it might be nice to have an equal footing with them.

The two shimmied and shuffled their way through all the cars parked like sardines. When Hound Dog came upon the car; he knew this car was it, especially since it had tinted windows like a limousine given his current legal predicament. A 2009 black Crown Victoria P-71 Police Interceptor without hubcaps, with flat black steel wheels that revealed the state-of-the-art disc brakes, and no decals or silly stickers. Another plus was that it looked lower to the ground than usual—similar to the Chevy Impalas of the mid-90s.

Slick started reviewing the statistics and heavy-duty features of the car, but Hound Dog wasn't really listening. He wanted to hear the engine. "Pop the hood and start it up." Fortunately, Slick always carried his keys on a giant key ring, so he was always ready for a willing customer. Plus, it was a lot safer than leaving them in the office with Marshmallow his cat.

The V8 engine started up without a hitch, and Hound Dog bent over to listen. It was music to his ears—eight cylinders clicking away like a sewing machine—sounded tight and in tune. But what he noticed under the hood made Hound Dog realize this was not your ordinary cop car; it was equipped with new turbo chargers, a performance exhaust system, and expensive shocks. Once Hound Dog was satisfied with the mechanics of the car he started doing his customary walk around. With the hood closed back down, he beat his fist on the car to see if it was solid or not. As he made his way around the car he noticed there weren't any antennae holes or scratches from where the lights are hooked up. Obviously, this cop car was a detective's car.

"So what's the story on this car?" asked Hound Dog.

"I'll shoot straight with you Hound Dog; this car was the detective that was killed a couple of months ago. The department doesn't like to hang on to cars of fallen cops, they think it's bad luck. I got it for a steal; no pun intended," answered Slick

"My Mark III is immaculate and you know it is my pride and joy. Let's do an even swap," offered Hound Dog.

Slick stammered for a second, but for some reason said, "Done deal." Slick had had difficulty trying to sell the car because people thought it was cursed, so he jumped at the chance to move it off of his lot. It was a fantastic car, and Slick knew that Hound Dog would not have any problems with it.

The two men shook hands and the deal was done. "Let's go sign all the paperwork and I will get Morris to move all the cars around so we can get it out and ready for you to roll." Hound Dog knew that the title and registration would take weeks to go through the system. This would give him some more time. And time was what he needed.

Chapter 7- Coffee Talk

Detectives Cole and Fortnight were at Ronnie's Diner on West 7th Street and Grand Avenue enjoying some coffee and reviewing their notes. The black juices invigorated their brain cells and they ran with their ideas from the interview with Al Porter.

"I'm intrigued by this Hound Dog figure. It looks like he was rehearsing a lot of hours these past two months," said Cole

"Maybe he was in the basement digging instead of rehearsing," responded Fortnight.

"I wonder where they put all of the dirt," said Cole.

"Why do you say 'they'? Do you think it was a crew of people digging?" asked Fortnight.

"This type of complex operation requires a lot of man hours. It would take one person digging for months and months, or a team at least a few weeks," answered Cole, "But the *more* important question is: where'd they put all the money?"

Fortnight's cell phone started ringing, and he said, "It's the chief; we better get it."

"Hey chief, what's up?" said Fortnight.

Chief Dixon was in no mood for chit-chat and did not appreciate Fortnight's casual manner, "I'll tell you what is up! Your time is up! I want to see some results soon before this case gets cold. This bank robbery is an embarrassment and heads are going to roll, so you and Barfsky better get on it." Fortnight knew when the chief gets this angry he starts spitting saliva, so he was glad that it was a phone call and not shouting and not the chief spitting in his face.

"Yes, sir, we're on it; you can count on us," said Fortnight as he straightened up in his chair. Cole could hear the chief yelling over the phone.

The chief didn't have time to talk any longer, the mayor was calling on the other line, "I've got to go; send me a situation report in an hour!" and hung up abruptly.

Fortnight put away his phone and said, "The chief is getting a lot of pressure from city hall already."

"Can you blame them? Some crooks are sitting on a load of cash, and we don't have a clue who they are," responded Cole.

"Read me the short-list of suspects. And then we can start knocking on some doors and asking questions," suggested Fortnight.

Cole looked over his smart phone, and read off his prime suspect, "Maurice Jackson, aka Hound Dog; it looks like he lives pretty close to here on West 5th Street and Summerset."

"Sounds good to me; let's blow this taco stand," responded Fortnight.

Chapter 8- Dumpster Diving

Detective Fortnight came to apartment 4B and knocked solidly on the door. There was no response. He knocked again, but louder. "Mr. Jackson, you in there?" Only silence greeted the detectives. "He must be out. Let's go see what we can find without a warrant."

On their way down the stairs they ran into one of Hound Dog's neighbors. "Excuse me; do you know where Maurice Jackson is?"

Responding in a gruff manner, "Who wants to know? You guys with the IRS?"

The detectives flashed their badges as if second nature, "I'm Detective Fortnight, and this is Detective Cole, Chicago Police Department."

"I'm a retired cop myself, my name's Johnny Handsome. I was a sergeant back in the day here in the 9th Precinct."

"We've heard a lot about you; pleasure to meet you sir." Responded Cole, but actually they had no idea who Johnny Handsome was, but thought they would try and see if it helped build some rapport.

"Were looking for Maurice Jackson; have you seen him lately?" asked Fortnight.

"You mean Hound Dog; I can't say that I have. He is a good friend of mine. I live in 4A across the hall from him with the Mrs.," answered Johnny.

"Can you tell us what kind of car he drives?" asked Cole.

"Oh sure, he drives a beautiful black Lincoln Mark III. It's a real sight to behold the way it glistens in the night. I can see it now." Closing his eyes with a narrow squint to keep an eye on the detectives and inhaling a deep breathe. "You know the cars that they had for that North Korean dictator's motorcade—just like Hound Dog's car. But of course Hound Dog's Mark III doesn't have the tacky chrome headlight covers…"

Fortnight interrupted the old man, "Have you noticed anything odd about Hound Dog recently? You know, coming back to his apartment at odd times of night, leaving early."

"Well, Hound Dog is a Blues man, so he is out at all hours of night playing his music. You should have heard his band play a few years ago at Rusty's on West 9th—they almost brought the house down with their loud music!" Laughing to himself, "Man, it was quite a sight to see that band up there jamming and a grooving."

Cole gave Fortnight the nod, and they cut the conversation off. "Thank you, sir, for your cooperation. Here are our cards; if you see Hound Dog come back home, please give us a call."

"Will do, will do," said Johnny as he put their cards in his shirt pocket.

And as the detectives parted company from the old cop, Johnny yelled down the stairwell to them, "Hey!" and pausing for effect, "You be careful out there," and gave them a wink.

A few minutes later the detectives were searching the garbage bin behind Hound Dog's apartment and found work trousers with dirt stains.

"Look at this, work gloves and a head lamp," said Cole, "In my book this looks like someone was working on a tunnel."

"Let's get a warrant on the double for the apartment and see what we can find inside," said Fortnight.

28

Fortnight took out a cigarette and lit up. He always did this when he was thinking about something clever. It made him feel like Sherlock Holmes. "Do we have a picture of our Mr. Hound Dog that we can start circulating to the beat cops? I have a sneaking suspicion that our prime suspect is on the move,"

Detective Cole chimed in, "Why don't we start calling him by his given name, Maurice William Jackson, it seems a lot more professional."

"Is that what his driver's license says?"

Chapter 9: New Identity

Hound Dog knew he would need a new identity to evade the police and make a new start. Resisting arrest was one thing, but his temper got the worst of him and he knew he could be charged with assault and battery against three police officers.

His new car felt fast, but he knew he couldn't open it up; he didn't want to draw attention to himself as he made his way to his next stop: Fredrico's Tamale Hut. Hound Dog knew the place was notorious for two things, mean salsa that could remove paint and Government Issue cards.

Another plus for the Crown Vic was its kicking sound system. Since Hound Dog doesn't own any CDs he regularly tuned into Chicago's finest Blues station, WBLU 108.1 FM. As was Hound Dog's custom he had to let the song finish; it was one of his peccadillos. This time it was one of Saw Tooth's classics, "Flatsville Curse":

> *Down on my luck till you came 'round,*
> *You made things go from bad to worse,*
> *Fightin' in the pool hall and some time in jail,*
> *You done gave me the Flatsville Curse.*

Saw Tooth could always jam out on the harmonica, something Hound Dog had never perfected.

> *Jail time ain't no fun, no sir, no sir,*
> *I'd rather be in the back of a hearse,*
> *Thirty-five days I spent with you in there,*
> *You done gave me the Flatsville Curse.*

30

"Stay in the car Sasha; I'll be right back," said Hound Dog as he got out of his new ride. All the running around and the adrenaline rush of fighting this morning had built up an appetite, so Hound Dog ordered a dozen beef tamales. While paying he slipped the cashier a one hundred dollar bill with the face up, the signal that he needed the full work up: driver's license, social security card, car insurance, and birth certificate.

"Do you want a CDL? It's an extra $50," asked the attendant.

"No thanks."

"What about a marriage certificate? We're running a special this month."

"No thanks."

"Write your height, weight, eye color and address on this ticket; your tamales will be right out," said the attendant performing her job with an eerie nonchalance.

Hound Dog took his best guesses and slid the paper back to the attendant.

"We always mark people as organ donors. Go get some condiments, and put your feet on the two foot prints," instructed the attendant.

Talking to himself Hound Dog said, "Wow, this is faster than the DMV."

At the condiments stand there was a small camera protruding from the wall above the verde salsa and the "en fuego" salsa. Hound Dog readied himself and tried to relax. He knew he was breaking the law for the second time in less than four hours. He tallied in his mind what the sentencing would add up to. Talking to himself, "Carry the one… Man, I've got to lay low for a time and hopefully I won't need to use these false documents unless I get in a real pinch."

By the time Hound Dog was done with half of the dozen tamales one of the forgers came out to present his work, saying "Here's your new identity, Mr. Bolotec."

"What kind of name is Bolotec? Sounds like some Taiwanese transistor maker."

"We thought it would have kind of a pseudo French-Aztec kind of feel," said the forger, shrugging his shoulders with a take or leave it type of attitude.

Hound Dog picked up his new driver's license, "Arnold Richard Bolotec. You got to be kidding me. It sounds fake."

The forger left the table, and Hound Dog took stock of the situation: "Well at least Sasha will enjoy eating the rest of the tamales; we've got to hit the road." Hound Dog stuffed the forged documents into his suit jacket and grumbled to himself, "What are they teaching kids these days in school—French-Aztec? You've got to be kidding me."

Chapter 10- Apartment Spotting

It was getting close to 4 pm by the time Detectives Cole and Fortnight got a search warrant and were ready to scour Hound Dog's apartment for clues. After knocking a few times they had the court appointed locksmith open the door.

"So this is a Blues man's abode," Fortnight said smugly as he readied the fingerprint kit. Fortnight was enamored with fingerprints so he always opted for the task and Cole always obliged.

Cole went over to the kitchen sink, "Looks like no one's been here since morning time; must have been a hearty breakfast," as he took note of the eggshells, cheddar cheese remnants, and the dirty dishes in the sink. From there he went to the small bedroom and took note of the orderly nature of everything.

After collecting some fingerprints Fortnight started scoping out Hound Dog's record collection, "This guy is quite the Blues collector. And look at this, Hound Dog's debut album. Get a load of this name, *Rushin' Vodka.*"

"Why don't you play it on the record player; it will give us a sense of what kind of guy he is," said Cole as he meticulously searched the bedroom closet for clues.

It had been a couple of decades since Fortnight had even touched a record player, but fortunately Hound Dog's Panasonic 9000 was automatic. The needle went right to the guide line and after a revolution and a half began to play side B's first song, "Nightmare."

Well, I woke up this mornin', and my head didn't feel right,
My mind was all messed up from the fright,

33

Because my dreams were a scary and spooky all night,

At this point the song has a guitar solo that is up-tempo and raw, but quickly returned to the song.

> *The first dream I didn't have no blanket and I nearly froze,*
> *The second dream I was hung up from my toes,*
> *But the third was the scariest, when I lost my nose.*

Right as the next song, "Train Tracks Gonna' Run You Down", was about to start Cole's cell phone started ringing. "Quick, turn the music off, the chief is on the horn."

"Hey boss, you got any leads for me to chase down?" asked Cole.

The chief was in his normal cantankerous mood and didn't appreciate being called "boss", so he let Cole have it like a drill sergeant yelling at a fresh Marine recruit at Paris Island. "You will address me as Chief Dixon. Do you understand me? If I hear you call me anything else, I am going to reach through this phone and choke you, myself."

Cole had to hold back the obvious comment that choking him through the cell phone was physically impossible, but he did the wise thing and held his tongue. The detective was tempted to put him on speaker phone so that Fortnight could listen to the rant. Everyone in the 9th Precinct didn't call the chief, "the hair-dryer" for nothing!

"Yes, Chief Dixon. I understand."

"Your situation report was pathetic. You must've been writing it while sitting on your rear-end sipping a cocoa-mocha latte; I want to see some results fast! Do we have an understanding?"

"Yes, Chief Dixon."

"The next time I hear from you; it better be something good," and with that Chief Dixon slammed his phone down.

Cole was still catching his breath after being chewed out. He didn't think the situation report was that bad, but the chief was looking for arrests and people sitting in the precinct jail. "Man, the chief is under some heavy pressure, and it seems like he is suffering from the CSI syndrome; his expectations are completely skewed."

"Check this out! This is another one of Hound Dog's albums entitled *Where's My Stimulus Check?* It's a group of songs all about the financial crisis of 2009," as Detective Fortnight unfolded the record album to examine the interior some papers fell to the floor. "These song titles are hilarious: 'Too Big to Fail', 'The Bank Done Me Wrong', 'No Chapter 11 for the Poor Man', 'Where's My Money', and 'What's a Man Gonna' Do When the Bank Done Ripped Him Off'. I could go on if you want me to, but I am getting the picture that Hound Dog has a grudge against the banking system. Maybe he is one of those Occupy Wall Street types."

Cole was half listening to the song titles as he peered down at the papers that had fallen out of the album cover and realized they were detailed architectural plans of the 3rd National Bank of Chicago building. "What do we have here? Looks like Hound Dog was quite the tunnel expert; this map gives all the details of the digging and placement of the main vault," said Detective Cole as he took out his tweezers to make sure that he didn't get any fingerprints on the evidence. "This ought to please the chief."

As the detectives were reveling over their new findings Hound Dog's telephone started ringing. Both detectives followed the ringing towards the kitchen area and found the phone beside an antiquated answering machine.

After two rings, Hound Dog's answering message started: "Hello, this is Hound Dog's home. If you are trying to reach Dr. Katz's office you have dialed the wrong number. Otherwise, you know what to do at the beep."

"Hey, Hound Dog, this is Slick. I guess you are still not home. Give me a call when you have a chance."

"What kind of name is Slick? Sounds interesting. Let's listen to his previous messages to find out more," suggested Detective Fortnight as he walked around the counter in front of the answering machine. As he gawked at the old device he said, "How do you work one of these things? It looks like it was made in the early 90s."

"I used to have one of those types with the tape; hit 'rewind' first, and when it is done rewinding click on 'play'. That ought to work," instructed Detective Cole.

The machine rewound and rewound for what seemed to the detectives an eternity until it finally halted with a loud thunk sound. Now it was time for the messages:

The first message was the following: "Hey Hound Dog, this is Larry down at Smarty's Pet and Feed. Just wanted to let you know that your bulk order of Lean and Mean Dog Chow came in and it's ready for you to pick it up." The detectives nodded at each other as if to communicate, "I'm glad we weren't attacked when we came into the apartment," or maybe it was more of a "He really keeps the place nice for having a dog in the apartment," type of nod.

The second message: "Mr." followed by an extremely long pause as if he was re-reading the name again and again, "Hound Dog?" questioning himself, "I'm with the Animal Protection Society of Greater Chicago, APSGA, and I was wondering…" Click, the message got cut off. Again, the detectives motioned at each other as if to say, "Spit it out man; you wasted too much time at the beginning."

Then came on Slick's previous message, the one the detectives really wanted to hear: "Hey Hound Dog, this is Slick. You must be rollin' in the dough now. We were vacuuming out your old car and found a big chunk of change in the Mark III. I will keep it safe for you. Come on by and pick it up when you have time. Over and out."

And then Slick's second message played again. The detectives looked at each other again and Detective Fortnight spoke first, "Looks like we need to go have a meeting with a Mr. Slick."

"My sentiments, exactly," said Detective Cole as he took the tape out of the answering machine for evidence.

Chapter 11- Drug Lord

It was late in the afternoon when his office phone rang.

"Hello," answered the boss.

The voice on the other end said, "This is your reminder that you still haven't paid me for what was taken from me. You are responsible for the debt and its growing. You have until Wednesday to return my stuff or pay up. I'll call you on Tuesday with the details."

"We need some more time to find it," the boss answered in a pathetic, yet sincere voice.

"I have been very patient with you, but you've done some very rash things that could potentially draw more attention to your operation. Just don't do anything stupid."

"Well, you know desperate times call for desperate actions," explained the boss.

"Look, I'm simply a businessman, but your time is coming to a close and I need the money in my hands soon. You understand?"

"Yes, I understand."

"Good, you're smart, and I like you. I'll give you a call on Sunday night to see if you have made up any ground on this problem."

"Thanks, hopefully we can get things squared away by then," he answered in a relieved voice.

Chapter 12- On the Interstate

Hound Dog was driving out of Chicago seeking the path of least resistance. Traffic was flowing on the interstate heading southeast towards Indiana, so Hound Dog followed the traffic and kept cruising down the road. In a roughly an hour his favorite radio station was out of range, so Hound Dog did what he did best—he sang the Blues:

> *I'm leaving you Chicago,*
> *Don't know when I'll be back home,*
> *Dark storms are blowing me out of town now,*
> *But someday I'll be back to see my friends.*

Hound Dog imagined a guitar solo that would fit this song and hummed to himself and added some twangs and tweets as best he could.

> *Don't exactly know where I am heading,*
> *But memories of you will still remain,*
> *Cause when you leave Chicago,*
> *You're always leaving friends.*

The road stretched out in front of him and he just kept driving and driving. The cruise control was engaged a mile or two below the speed limit so as not to draw attention or get pulled over. The tamales Hound Dog had for lunch and the stresses of the day had ruined his appetite for dinner, so he just kept moving further from Chicago. Sasha would whine if she needed to get out of the car, but she looked content to ball herself up in the backseat.

The miles rolled on and on like an escalator. Hound Dog felt good; he was putting distance between himself and his legal troubles.

Suddenly Hound Dog tensed when he saw lights flash in his rear view mirror—his heartbeat picked up and he felt his pulse pound. "Take deep breaths, Hound Dog," he said to himself to help him keep his composure. Fortunately the patrol car sped by him and was concerned with some other matter. "That was a close one, Sasha."

Sasha stirred from her sleep, lifted her head and let out a groan as if to say, "Chill out."

"If wolves could talk, what would they say?" Hound Dog asked himself, knowing perfectly well that Sasha was listening. Hound Dog was half-optimistic that one of these days Sasha would talk to him like some beast from Narnia. "I know what Sasha would say: 'Give me some red meat; I'm hungry.' That's what she would be talking about all the time. It would be non-stop: steak, prime rib; Oh, I know… lamb chops!" Hound Dog chuckled to himself.

Hound Dog was realizing a major drawback of the Crown Vic was the CD player. Hound Dog was an avid eight-track connoisseur; he was an expert at repairing the tapes as well. It had been awhile since Hound Dog had been out of radio reception of WBLU and without at least a small portion of his eight-track collection. His landlord will probably put everything out on the street when he misses his rent at the end of the month. *Maybe I could send him a money order*, Hound Dog thought to himself. His next thought was the cops that he assaulted this morning exacting their revenge by tearing his apartment to pieces. *Maybe there will be nothing left after they smash everything and sell the records at some public auction.*

Ahead the skies were darkening; rain showers were brewing ahead. Hound Dog thought it better to pull over now and let Sasha relieve herself before it gets too wet outside. "Wake up Sasha," he said as he pulled the car over to the side of the road into the emergency lane. The car shuddered as it went over the wake-up ruts, and then there was a loud pop when the back right tire blew out.

"Man! I really don't need this right now!" getting out of the car and opening the rear door for Sasha to get out for some fresh air. "Surely Slick has a good spare tire for me," said Hound Dog with baited breath as he popped the trunk. And there it was—a fresh and full size tire. Hound Dog deplored those spare donuts as lame excuses for tires that you can only drive for 5 miles or less to the service station.

The rain started to fall and he looked to see a sheet of rain coming his way—about a mile away. Hound Dog couldn't afford to stay on the road any longer than necessary. At least he could keep the backseat dry since all the water would shed off of Sasha's coat, and he yelled for her to jump in the backseat.

Hound Dog started unscrewing the bolt that kept the spare tied down and started scanning the rest of the trunk for the tire wrench and jack. He didn't see the jack, so after he laid the tire beside the blown tire he started searching more intently.

"Okay, Slick, don't fail me now… Where is it? It's got to be around here somewhere." Hound Dog thought back to a previous car where the jack was hidden above the front passenger wheel well, but he thought that was entirely nonsensical. Hound Dog kept prodding and hitting portions of the trunk. "It's gotta' be around here, somewhere.

What's this?" as Hound Dog watched the automated motion of a section of the trunk start moving on its own.

"Holy Pablo Escobar! This can't be happening to me."

Hound Dog stood there dumbfounded for a moment staring at 36 bricks of cocaine neatly and precisely packed to fit in a hidden compartment of the trunk. Hound Dog was so flabbergasted that he didn't notice when the wall of rain hit him at full force. All he said to himself was, "I'm driving a car full of cocaine. My life is over."

Chapter 13- The Confessional

Night had fallen in Chicago and the rains from the east had washed the streets clean and brought relief from the summer heat. Three men entered the old Catholic church on West 19th and Fitzhugh, St. Francis Catholic Church, and they made their way to the confessional. One entered in while the other two men waited in the pews and kept a look out.

"I don't come to confessionals that often, boss," commented the lead thug.

"Bless you my son," was the response from the priest's station behind the wicker enclosed window.

This took the confessor off guard, "Is that you, boss?"

"I'm just having fun with you. You guys did a good job this morning. Hound Dog is on the run and the cops have him pegged as the prime suspect; his flight only makes him look all the more guilty. It must have been quite a scuffle this morning."

"We thought a Blues magician would be a pushover, but he fights like a man possessed. After I put the pepper mace in his face he went berserk," replied the confessing thug.

"Now you understand why he was the perfect candidate to pin the bank heist on; he's got in scrapes before because of his temper," explained the boss.

"I had quite a headache after he whacked me with the guitar; he didn't even give me a chance to fake being knocked out," replied the thug.

"I guess it's an occupational hazard of impersonating a policeman," responded the boss dryly.

"And boss, we planted the evidence in his apartment dumpster, and even inside his apartment just as you directed," said the confessor.

"What about the car?" asked the boss.

"Oh yeah, we stuck $10k under his seat. Those old Lincoln locks are a cinch to crack."

"Excellent," and there was a pause as the speaker acting as priest wanted to emphasize the change in topic, "Let's talk about your other job: the search for Canton's cocaine. Did you find anything at the detective's home?"

"No, but we sure did smash the place," giving a slight chuckle to communicate he was really pleased with himself, "We even gained access to his storage facility and searched it thoroughly—still no coke."

"Have you found that crooked cop's car, yet? My bet is that he held his cards closely."

"No, we haven't found it, but we are still looking," answered the criminal.

"Good, keep up the search; Canton wants his payment by next Wednesday. Speaking of money, your bonuses are under the pew right outside the confessional; I will be in touch."

Chapter 14- Truck Stop

It was late and Hound Dog was soaked to the bone. He pulled up to Bertha and Fred's Truck Stop. When he saw the road sign, "Eat Here and Get Gas", Hound Dog knew he had to pull over. Sasha stayed in the car, and Hound Dog cracked the windows ever so slightly so she could have enough ventilation without allowing the rain to come inside the car.

"Let me see what I can get you, girl," said Hound Dog.

Hound Dog knew he needed to find a place with dog food; finding a pet store or a grocery store would be one of tomorrow's tasks. Maybe Hound Dog could find work in one of the rural, low-key factories around here.

Bertha and Fred's Truck Stop was well-lit inside and it almost hurt Hound Dog's eyes to look around such a brightly lit place. He used the restroom facilities and noticed that the mirror was covered in graffiti. People must have had a nagging feeling to rebel against the small sign above the sink that read, "Do NOT write on the mirror." The mirror was covered by all sorts of comments and tags, lots of "Crypto wuz here", "Tommy rocks the house!", and "Polish Revolution 2012".

The next challenge for Hound Dog was navigating the air dryer that about blew his hands off as it made the flesh on his hands flap and vibrate. The decal read "Warp Drive 6000". He could imagine the dryer frightening small children with its shrieking blasts of hot air. At least it helped Hound Dog dry his clothes off quickly.

Hound Dog found the hot food section and was wise to avoid all the fried foods sitting under the heat lamps; he had been burned once before eating an old, decrepit fried fish and chips; he promised himself to avoid that experience again at all costs. Hound Dog thought to himself, *I guess premade, prepackaged, permafrost pizzas will have to do for tonight. Sasha loves pizza!*

At the counter when he was checking out Hound Dog asked the attendant, "Do you know how to get people to stop writing on the men's restroom mirror?"

"No, I don't. But it's a real pain in the neck to clean," answered the attendant as if she loathed the chore of cleaning Marks-A-Lot off the mirror every week.

"Take the sign 'do NOT write on the mirror' sign down; people have a persistent urge to rebel against rules like that," said Hound Dog, "Especially when they are in private." When the words came out of Hound Dog's mouth his own conscience was pricked, and he thought to himself, *Look at yourself running from the law!*

"Thanks, I'll pass that on to the manager; it drives him crazy when people do it," answered the attendant.

Hound Dog gathered up his items and was about to walk out the door, but turned to ask, "Oh, by the way, do you know of a good, yet inexpensive motel in this area?"

Pointing south she answered, "Yeah, head down the state highway for about 20 miles, and you'll see the Stardust Motel on the right-hand side. Tell'em Jackie sent you and they'll take real good care of you."

"Thanks for the tip," replied Hound Dog.

Chapter 15- Breakfast at Tiffany's

The next morning Hound Dog and Sasha woke up late at the Stardust Motel that the gas station attendant had recommended. The motel management must really be fond of Jackie, because mentioning her name landed Hound Dog and his wolf in the honeymoon suite. The room was a Saint Valentine's theme: completely decked out in red satin sheets, shams, pillow cases, drapes, and even had a complimentary plastic red rose in a red vase. Even the towels were red with embroidered pink hearts. Sasha's black coat stood out in stark contrast to the red shag carpet with a giant arrow shooting cupid woven into the middle of the room.

Hound Dog was famished, but most of all his mouth was parched from eating a super salty pizza the night before from the truck stop. Fortunately, the motel was a short drive from a small diner that serves breakfast and lunch. Outside the weather was nice and clear after the rain storms, so Hound Dog left the front windows down for Sasha to enjoy the day. Plus, he needed to let the front driver's seat dry from last night's drenching.

Hound Dog entered the diner and didn't see anyone around but another customer that was seated in a booth by the windows. Hound Dog decided to take a seat on the other side of the diner since the other customer didn't seem pleased to see Hound Dog come through the front door. As Hound Dog took a seat he wondered to himself, *Where in Indiana am I?* He had missed seeing any signs on the small state highway into town, and Hound Dog thought to himself, *Welcome to Hoosierville, Indiana, birth place of Wyatt Herb and Wayne Newton.*

Hound Dog was admiring all the decorations and old photos on the diner walls. He liked this place; it had a history. There was a framed dollar bill, probably the first one from a paying customer. Yet, Hound Dog's appraisal of the place stopped suddenly when the most beautiful woman that he had ever seen came through the kitchen doorway. She was carrying breakfast over to the gruff looking customer. Upon seeing her Hound Dog stood up from his chair out of respect as if the Queen of England had entered the room. She smiled; she must have been used to having guys fall over themselves when they saw her.

She delivered the food and came back to take Hound Dog's drink order, "Good morning. What would you like to drink this morning?"

"I'll have some coffee, please," said Hound Dog, "And can I ask you a question?"

"Sure," she replied.

"Where am I?" asked Hound Dog.

"You're at Breakfast at Tiffany's," she answered thinking it odd that he would ask such an obvious question.

"Um… I mean what town is this?" said Hound Dog embarrassed that he had asked such a stupid question, but he was still in awe of her shocking beauty. And he felt nervous even looking into her beautiful eyes.

"Oh, this is Santiago, Indiana," she replied.

Hound Dog laughed it off, "Gotcha', thanks."

"No problem. I'll go get your coffee and be right back to take your breakfast order."

Hound Dog was wondering to himself, *How she could be so kind; she could have totally bashed him for asking such a stupid question!* She was a good-hearted woman and Hound Dog was already smitten. Hound Dog didn't like to eat at places where the wait staff was rude and obnoxious; he really didn't see why some restaurants actually enjoyed the notoriety for being rude to their customers. Maybe they attract masochists that are looking for a good time.

Then quickly Hound Dog's mind returned to thoughts of the most gorgeous woman in the entire world. *How could it be? Of all the places, who would have known that the most attractive woman in the world lives in Santiago, Indiana*, thought Hound Dog, *I wonder if she likes wolves*. Hound Dog was already getting ahead of himself. First he had to figure out how to get to know this woman and at least find out know her name. *Does she have a wedding ring?*

Hound Dog knew that she would be coming back to take his breakfast order and he didn't want to be a dead beat customer, so he looked over the menu quickly. But before glancing over the pancake section Hound Dog was stirred from his thoughts when the gruff customer started barking out some complaint, "Hey Tiff! These eggs are rotten!"

When returning from the kitchen carrying a coffee pot in her hand she approached the man and said, "Let me take a look."

After examining the eggs, she told him, "Nothing's wrong with the eggs; they're fine. I don't know what you are talking about, Larry," she replied kindly. She tried to play it off and give him an out, "Maybe you thought you saw something."

"Well I think the eggs taste like dog vomit and I ain't paying for them!" said Larry.

Hound Dog didn't like this guy talking to her that way and yelled over to him, "Watch your language when you are talking to a lady," Hound Dog could hardly believe he was talking.

"You'll keep your pie-hole shut if you know what's good for you!" yelled back Larry from his booth. And grabbing Tiffany's arm he said, "I can treat her any way I like!" and proceeded to shake her around.

"Stop Larry; your hurting me!" she exclaimed as she tried to draw back her arm.

"You better unhand her, right now," said Hound Dog in the calmest voice he could muster, but his mood tie was already starting to change from blue to red. He knew this situation could go south and get really ugly.

"UN-hand her? You must be a real Shakespeare!" Larry said as he kept a tight grip on Tiffany's arm. "What you going to do about it, boy genius?"

Hound Dog made his best attempt to diffuse the situation from his seat some 20 feet away from him, "C'mon man, you can let go of her arm and she can get back to her work."

But Larry was looking for trouble, so he just repeated his question with added bravado, "What are you going to do about it? Ain't no smarty pants gonna' tell me what to do. I have a black belt."

This set Hound Dog off and "Voodoo Chile" by Jimi Hendrix started playing in Hound Dog's mind. It was go time! Hound Dog got out of his chair and said, "Yeah, a black belt in stupidity. I'll throw you out of here; that's what I'll do!" as he walked towards Larry and Tiffany.

"I'd like to see that," laughed Larry as he stood up and made a rather imposing stance. Larry weighed over 260 pounds at six foot four—stout as a professional linebacker. Larry proceeded to taunt Hound Dog, "Why you sticking up for a no good..." but before he could finish his derogatory remarks towards Tiffany, Hound Dog had closed Larry's mouth abruptly with his thumb and pointer finger protruding from a clinched fist into a painful pressure point under Larry's chin. With his left hand Hound Dog freed Larry's grip on Tiffany's arm by forcing Larry's thumb back into his own knuckle; this gave Larry the sensation that his thumb was about to break in two if he didn't let go.

After Tiffany was free, Hound Dog wrenched Larry's right arm behind his back by using his right thumb for leverage. This sudden movement exposed Larry's right side, and Hound Dog jabbed him with his thumb to help show him that he was in charge before putting his thumb firmly behind a pressure point under Larry's ear—this produced an instant and painful headache. Hound Dog moved the big brute towards the front door and forced him outside and out over the steps. Larry landed with a heavy thud on the blacktop.

Only Larry's truck and Hound Dog's old cop car were in the parking lot, so by process of elimination Hound Dog told him, "You better get in your truck and get out of here. And don't come back!"

But Larry had other designs; he had just been humiliated by some stranger in a black suit with an odd colored tie. Larry went to the back of his truck to find a crow bar and started walking over to Hound Dog's Crown Vic.

"I wouldn't do that if I were you!" cautioned Hound Dog.

Larry ignored him and took a swing at the Crown Victoria's front windshield. Fortunately, the crooked detective had replaced the front windshield with Plexiglas, so the crow bar just glanced off the windshield and didn't shatter. But the abrupt thud alerted Sasha and triggered her attack mode. Larry didn't have a chance to swing twice at the car because Sasha flew out of the open passenger window and her teeth crunched Larry's hand like a stale chocolate chip cookie. Hound Dog could hear the bones breaking to bits, and he gained no satisfaction in Larry's pain.

Hound Dog repressed the urge to tell him, "I told you so."

Larry screamed in agony as he dropped the crow bar and fell to the ground, "Aargh! My hand is broken!"

"She doesn't take kindly to people trying to smash her windows; it disrupts her beauty sleep," said Hound Dog as Sasha stood over him with his mutilated hand in her mouth. Larry was fortunate that the wolf was exercising constraint and didn't attack further.

"Get your mutt off of me!" yelled Larry hysterically.

"Sasha, release," said Hound Dog calmly, and Sasha came over to Hound Dog's side to be rewarded with a, "Good girl; now sit."

In the distance Hound Dog heard police sirens. "You better clear out of here before the cops come and arrest you for public stupidity," said Hound Dog guessing that Larry wasn't too popular with the local law enforcement crowd. Larry trudged off to his pick-up with his injured hand cradled by his other hand. He hopped in, and had trouble starting his car with his left hand. To have the final word Larry yelled back, "You ain't seen the last of me, city-boy!" as his pick-up truck squealed out of the parking lot.

Hound Dog had to fight the urge to run, himself. The sound of the sirens made his body tense, but when he turned around and saw Tiffany at the doorway there was no way he was leaving. He would be happy to spend a night in the county jail fighting for her honor. *Mr. Bolotec* would have to be a man of courage.

Chapter 16- Slick's First Interview

Around the time Hound Dog was starting to argue with Larry in northern Indiana, Detectives Fortnight and Cole were driving into Slick's Used Car Palace and Garage back in Chicago. When Slick saw the black Crown Vic he thought for a moment that it was Hound Dog returning for the money that he had left under the Mark III's front seat. This assessment quickly changed when he saw two guys come out of the car, and neither one looked like Hound Dog. They looked like cops by the way they held themselves and the way they scoped out their surroundings. In Slick's assessment they looked on edge, but also self-assured.

Slick was confident that he didn't have any stolen cars on his lot, so he wondered what they wanted as he got up to meet them outside. Maybe they are in the market to buy a car he thought optimistically (because you've got to be an optimist if you are in the car business). But when they pointed at him to come talk outside Slick got nervous again and met them with random sales pitch questions: "Can I help you gentlemen? Are you in the market for a gently used luxury car?" and finally, "Something for the Mrs.?"

Fortnight and Cole weren't amused and flashed their badges and said they would be the ones asking the questions. Before arriving at Slick's the two detectives agreed that they wouldn't directly bring up the cash that Slick had mentioned in his phone message, but they would say they saw Hound Dog's car in the lot.

"Come into my office and we can talk in there," replied Slick, knowing that he would be more at ease in his office and out of earshot of the other employees. They all entered Slick's cramped office that was chocked full of racing trophies and pictures of racecars with Slick at the wheel. Cole was a car buff so he examined all the pictures and let Fortnight takes the lead on the questions. Not that he was being aloof; Cole was still listening intently for any faltering or juggling of words—dead giveaways that they were dealing with a liar. Plus, if Slick gave any resistance to the questioning, he could always jump in and act like the angry "bad" cop that won't take no for an answer.

Fortnight started the questions with a little background, "We noticed that you have a Lincoln Mark III that used to be owned by a Blues musician named Maurice "Hound Dog" Jackson; when did that vehicle come into your possession?"

"Oh, just yesterday morning," replied Slick.

"What kind of car did he trade the Mark III in for?" asked Fortnight.

"He got a real deal on a used cop car—one of the best Crown Vics I've ever seen. Quite a smooth ride and fast as lightning," replied Slick. And when Slick starts talking about speed he gets excited, "I took that car for a test spin over at the track one day, and it got up to 150 miles per hour like it was just getting started. Man let me tell you, it had plenty of juice with those turbos on it!"

Inquisitively, Fortnight asked his next question, "You said this was a former police department car, do you have the paperwork on it?"

Slick answered, "Oh sure, let me find it," as he shuffled some papers and moved Marshmallow off his messy desk. "I have my own feline secretary," said Slick as he found the old title that used to belong to the Chicago Police Department, "Here it is," handing it over to Fortnight.

It didn't take Fortnight long to confirm his suspicions, the previous owner's custom Illinois plates, IMNUM1(I'm number 1)—was all he needed to see to know that it was Detective Kartow's Crown Vic. Everyone in the department knew he was more crooked than a road in the Swiss Alps. Rumor had it that he was gaming both sides until the drug lords finally killed him. Kartow poured his extra cash in to his "work" car to make it more like a Porsche 911 with a Ford body. There were even rumors that he had the car fitted with armor to protect the driver and passenger sections.

Fortnight set the old title on the desk so it could catch the sunlight coming in through the windows and took a couple of pictures of it with his smart phone.

Cole chimed in and asked, "Did Hound Dog say why he was trading in his Mark III?"

Slick answered, "He said he needed a car that got better gas mileage."

"That sounds reasonable. Any idea why he picked out the Crown Vic?" asked Detective Cole.

"It was the first car I showed him and he liked it. We signed the paperwork and he was off lickety-split," replied Slick.

"Did he say where he was going?" asked Cole.

"No he didn't, he just drove off," answered Slick.

"How long have you known Hound Dog?" asked Fortnight, rejoining the conversation after his contemplations on Kartow. He was hopeful that Slick would say something about the cash he had found in the Mark III.

"Oh, I don't know, about ten or so years; I sold him the Mark III then, and he brought it in here for regular servicing; we became friends. He stops in periodically just to shoot the breeze," replied Slick, "What gives? Is Hound Dog in some kind of trouble?"

"We'll just say he is under investigation; here are our cards—give us a call if you see Hound Dog. We need to talk to him about some things," answered Cole.

"Did he get in trouble for fighting again? I know he has quite a reputation for that temper of his," Slick volunteered.

This raised the detectives' antennae.

The detectives got back in their car and debriefed on their interview with Slick.

Cole spoke first: "Sounds like we've got a real fighter on our hands."

"We'll have to keep that in mind when we make his arrest," responded Fortnight.

"I didn't see any weapons in his apartment, so I don't think he is armed. But we won't take any chances."

Chapter 17- The Sheriff of Santiago

Hound Dog recounted the situation in his mind as the approaching sirens were getting louder: *I just threw a guy out of diner in Indiana; my wolf crushed the guy's hand after he tried to break my windshield, and then he drove off. And now the cops were coming.*

Tiffany came outside to console Hound Dog, and she even patted Sasha on the head. Talking to Sasha in a puppy dog kind of voice she said, "You're such a brave doggy, taking care of your master's car; good doggy." And to Hound Dog she said, "I called my daddy after you threw him out."

"I guess your dad called the police," replied Hound Dog.

Tiffany answered quickly and nonchalantly, "Why, he's the sheriff."

A giant gulp came into Hound Dog's mouth and he stammered out a reply, "Oh... G-good," and after quickly regaining his composure, "They sure do have quick response times here in Santiago."

It was about that moment when the sheriff's squad car came to an abrupt stop in the diner parking lot and the sheriff got out of the car to run over to see his beloved daughter, "Are you alright, Tiffany?"

"Yes, daddy, I'm alright," and turning towards Hound Dog, "And this is the man that freed my arm and threw Larry out of the diner."

Sticking out a firm hand to shake, the sheriff said, "Thanks for standing up for my daughter. Let me buy you a cup of coffee inside. It's the least I can do."

Hound Dog shook the sheriff's hand, and didn't know what to say, so he just said, "My pleasure, and I'll gladly take you up on your offer." Hound Dog put Sasha back into the car, and as the three of them turned to go into the diner Hound Dog thought to himself, *This is crazy. I'm having coffee with the local sheriff while I'm supposed to be on the run from the law.*

The sheriff was visibly proud of Hound Dog for protecting Tiffany and throwing Larry out of the restaurant, "Come take a seat up here at the counter," talking to Hound Dog, "And let's have some coffee," as he poured some into the cups that Tiffany had provided. "I'm sorry, I didn't even ask your name," said the sheriff as he patted Hound Dog on the back.

This was a moment of truth for Hound Dog, what was he to do? He couldn't say his name was Hound Dog, and definitely couldn't lie to the father of the most beautiful woman in the world and say his name was Bolo-*whatever*. So Hound Dog just did the most rational thing he could do: he stalled out by taking a really long sip of coffee.

"My name is…" started Hound Dog, but was interrupted by the Sheriff's radio blurting out, "16-22, we've got a 93-9er, all cars report to the scene at Harvest and Main."

"Tiffany, I've got to go; I love you," said the Sheriff as he took his last gulp and started moving towards the door, "Enjoy that coffee, you earned it."

"I love you too, daddy," Tiffany said as he left the diner.

Chapter 18- Back at Tri-City Records

After the detectives left, Slick was worried about his friend, Hound Dog, so he called Tri-City Records to see if he was there.

Jeff "Lightning" Watkins answered the phone, "Good morning, Tri-City Records here."

"Hey, is this Lightning?" asked Slick.

"You better believe it. Who's this?"

"This is Slick from Slick's Used Car Palace and Garage."

"Hey Slick, you know I've been meaning to bring my car in for some work. But what can I do for you?" said Lightning.

"Well, yesterday Hound Dog traded in his Mark III, and I wanted to see if he was at Tri-City Records."

"I guess you didn't know Hound Dog is in trouble. He is on the run from the law for fighting with some cops yesterday."

"What? Well that explains it, he was really quick in picking the first car I showed him and then he was off once the paperwork was done," explained Slick.

"Yeah, it's a real shame; he's never been able to keep his temper in check," said Lightning.

"You know what? I'm going to have to go; I've got some customers to deal with," explained Slick.

"Alright, you take care," replied Lightning.

"Will do, and I'll look out for you to bring in your car soon. Take care."

Chapter 19- Late Breakfast

Hound Dog was polishing off a tall stack of pancakes and sausages. He was relishing the maple syrup dribbling over the sausages. Now Hound Dog was truly smitten because he had always contended that food is the sixth love language; the perfect combination of the other five love languages (even if words of affirmation really doesn't work into the mix).

"So what's your name?" asked Tiffany.

"Maurice Jackson, but all my friends in Chicago call me Hound Dog."

"I like the name Maurice, and I've never had a friend with such an interesting nickname."

"Pleased to meet you, Tiffany," sticking out his hand to shake hers.

"How did you like the pancakes?" asked Tiffany.

"They were fantastic; what did you put in them?"

"It's a secret family recipe."

"C'mon, you can tell me; I promise," crossing his heart with his index fingers, "And I won't tell anyone that you told me."

"Prunes," she said slyly.

"No way, you're joking."

Tiffany laughed and said, "Yes way," as she made her way back to the kitchen.

Hound Dog sat there contemplating to himself how in the world he was going to be able to stay in Santiago to get to know Tiffany better. *I guess I could always come back for lunch.* But when she came back, he took a more direct approach: "Tiffany, I know we just met each other, and I don't even know your last name, but can I take you out for dinner?"

"Um… Maurice… We barely met," she said as she thought aloud since his question had taken her off guard, "I know you are a nice guy, but I don't know what my dad will say."

"I'm not asking him out on a date."

"As you can imagine my dad is very protective of me; he has to approve of any man that wants to take me on a date first," said Tiffany.

"Okay, would tonight be a good time to come see him?"

"I think so, he should be home tonight; how about you come by around eight o'clock. That way he can fully unwind from the stresses of the day."

"Great; I've got to run some errands to take care of Sasha, and some other things, so I will see you tonight."

Tiffany and Hound Dog parted company and she told him where she lives and the best place to find dog food and other sundry items. As Hound Dog got back into the car he was so elated he was worried he would bump into the headliner of the car. Hound Dog couldn't contain himself, he had to verbalize his good news, "Sasha, I've got a date with an angel tonight at eight!"

Hound Dog started up the car and was so happy he came up with a little song to express his elation:

> *What's a man gonna' do when he on the run from the law,*
> *And he knows he is fallin' for the sheriff's daughter,*
> *I can't leave her, I can't kick her out of my heart,*
> *But her daddy just might throw me in the slammer!*

I got a date with the sheriff's daughter,
But she doesn't know I'm on the wrong side of the law,
What's a man to do when he loves somebody,
But doesn't want to go to jail…

"We're going to have to work on that last part, Sasha," said Hound Dog as they drove down the road in search of the local grocery store, "It's funny how this situation is causing me to sing the Blues even though I am falling in love."

Chapter 20- Catching up with the Detectives

"I think our man, Hound Dog, has flown the coop," said Detective Cole as they knocked on Hound Dog's apartment door.

The locksmith knew that was his signal to open the door. Detectives Cole and Fortnight were back again to see if they could track him down. The finger prints hadn't matched anything from the bank's vault. The perpetrator or perpetrators had been extra careful to cover their tracks, so all the finger prints at the crime scene were bank employees.

The detectives had put out notices for the Chicago police to be on the lookout for Hound Dog and started posting his picture in the surrounding precincts.

The detectives entered and left the door open as they went in; they did not expect to stay long.

"Let's see if we can find an address book or something to help us pick up the trail; he might have some relatives or friends that are willing to hide him for a while," said Cole.

"Sounds good," responded Fortnight as he made his way to check out Hound Dog's record collection. He was more interested in the record player, and made quick work to put on one of Saw Tooth's classic albums—*Heartbreakin' Blues*. The first song, "Shotgun Sunrise", was a classic that went something like this:

When I woke up that morning,
I knew it was gonna' be a bad, bad day,
Because a shotgun sunrise only means one thing,
It's time to break the rocks.

Dreams are done and buried,

Only heartache and misery greet you,
And the day is just beginning,
When a shotgun sunrise starts your day.

Oh, how I hate that ugly shotgun,
Cold steel and cruel hate,
It cares nothing for your life,
Ain't nothing worse than a shotgun sunrise.

"Man, that was depressing," said Fortnight.

"That's why they call it the Blues; now get busy searching that bookshelf over there." answered Cole.

Then a voice at the doorway started the detectives, "Hey, Hound Dog!"

Cole and Fortnight instinctively went for their holsters.

"Hold on there, Yosemite Sam, it's just me," said Johnny Handsome, Hound Dog's neighbor, "I saw the door open and I thought Hound Dog was back."

The detectives relaxed their guard seeing the old cop at the doorway.

Chapter 21- Meeting the Father

"Well Sasha, this must be Tiffany's home, the sheriff's car is parked out front," said Hound Dog. "You know I'm going to have to stop talking to you when Tiffany and I are hanging out tonight; it's called a date." Hound Dog couldn't leave Sasha behind at the Star Dust Motel's honeymoon suite—she might get bored and tear the place to pieces. And Hound Dog would be forced to use all of his emergency money replacing red satin pillow covers and cupid ornaments.

Hound Dog had to park on the street since the driveway was full of police cars. This made Hound Dog nervous, *What are all these cop cars here for? Looks like a cop convention or something.* Hound Dog looked back at Sasha in the car to say good-bye just in case this was a trap; *Maybe they are all here to arrest me.*

He felt really awkward as he remembered that he didn't even know Tiffany's last name, and Hound Dog cursed himself, "I must be in love; I didn't even get her last name." Fortunately it was election season in Santiago and there was a sign in the front yard that had been blocked by all of the other squad cars, "Re-Elect Sheriff Baker" was plain to see.

When Hound Dog reached out to ring the doorbell the front door flew open and a man inside gave a hearty welcome, "You must be *Hound Dog*, come on in!" Hound Dog was a little stunned, to see a state trooper greet him, but he proceeded through the doorway.

"I'm Rick Baker, one of Tiffany's big brothers. Dad called us all in to come and meet the man that is interested in courting our little sister," said Rick as he presented a good, extra-firm handshake. As they shook hands Rick drew Hound Dog closer and whispered in his ear softly,

"You mess with my sister and I'll kick your tail all the way back to Chicago."

Like some multiple personality case, Rick shifted back in to mister nice guy mode, "Come and meet the rest of the family," said with a hearty slap on the back that left a stinging sensation.

"Hi, I'm Roger Baker," said another man decked out in law enforcement garb of Santiago's finest.

"Nice to meet you, you can call me Maurice or Hound Dog."

Roger took Hound Dog's hand for a handshake and came around to give him a hug. This brought Hound Dog's right ear close to Roger's mouth and he whispered, "You hurt my sister and I'll sick the hounds of hell on you." As they separated, Roger smiled and gave Hound Dog a warm introduction to the last brother, Josiah.

Josiah took a little while to get up out of the low recliner in the living room, because when he stood up he was built like a Russian Greco-Roman wrestler. Hound Dog thought to himself, *He must have to special order his uniform.*

"Nice to meet you, Josiah," said Hound Dog as he stuck out his hand.

Josiah didn't shake hands he just gave Hound Dog a big welcoming bear hug and whispered, "You even touch my sister…" and with a jolting squeeze to the ribs for emphasis, "and I will break you in half."

Hound Dog felt like his heart was going to explode, and with the last remnants of breath whispered, "Nice to meet you, too."

The sheriff just shouted from the dining room, "Come on back here, Maurice." The three brothers took their seats in the living room and awaited further orders. They had delivered their sincere threats of intense pain and now it was time for Hound Dog to go meet Tiffany's father. Hound Dog discovered the sheriff cleaning a large caliber sniper rifle on the dining table.

"Good evening, Sheriff Baker," said Hound Dog.

As he entered he noticed that the sheriff had Creedence Clearwater Revival's "Rollin' On The River" playing from a small radio in the room. Hound Dog was feeling more at ease already.

"Evening Maurice, glad you could come over tonight for a chat," said the sheriff as he applied oil to the firing mechanism. "Have you ever seen one of these up close? It's a Barrett M82."

Hound Dog, not being too fond of firearms said, "That's the largest gun I've ever seen in person."

"This is a RIFLE!" barked the sheriff like a drill sergeant. It was one of the sheriff's pet peeves.

Hound Dog, thought to himself, *Strike one! This is not starting off well. Now after the three musketeers is he trying to threaten me, too?*

"I'm not much one for rifles and such," replied Hound Dog.

"Well you can see the door!" said the sheriff laughing. "I'm just playing with you; come take a seat. I've got some paperwork for you to fill out."

Hound Dog sat down in front of a small stack of papers with a pen. At the top of the first page read: "APPLICATION TO DATE MY BELOVED DAUGHTER" (See Appendix A).

Hound Dog started reading over it and was quite shocked by the intimidating questions and conditions and threats of physical harm listed in the application. By the third page Sheriff Baker couldn't contain his laughter any longer and said, "Don't worry, I was just pulling your chain!"

"Sheriff, you're quite the joker," said Hound Dog as he was relieved he didn't have to fill out the paperwork and sign it in blood after pricking his finger with the rusty, Tetanus infected pin that was attached. Plus, he didn't have any passport photos on hand.

"Yeah, I like to crack a good joke every now and then," and then the sheriff's demeanor changed, and he said, "But there are some things I am dead serious about." And the sheriff looked at Hound Dog with cold steel eyes that were searching and serious. He continued, "My daughter, Tiffany, is a real treasure. And she is more beautiful on the inside than you know now."

"I can believe that," chimed in Hound Dog.

Quickly the sheriff asked Hound Dog a pointed question, "Have you ever heard of the curse of beauty?"

"No, I didn't know it was a curse to be beautiful," answered Hound Dog, "Isn't everyone trying to be beautiful?"

"That's the curse; every woman is envious of the beautiful woman, and every man wants to exploit or take advantage of her," explained the sheriff.

"You know I've never thought of it that way," admitted Hound Dog.

"Let me back up. Before Tiffany's mom passed away, she made all the Baker men make a promise to protect her darling Tiffany from the curse. I've no doubt you caught a hint of that as you met my three sons."

Hound Dog rubbed his ribs and said, "Yeah, I'm still recovering."

"Well count yourself lucky. Sometimes they won't let Tiffany's suitors come through the front door. They must have been impressed that you stood up for her this morning," said the sheriff. "And I've seen them throw guys out that shook their hand the wrong way, or even looked at Tiffany with lust in their eyes."

Hound Dog was starting to feel pretty happy about himself that he had made it this far—he had made it past the gate keepers. But that's when the sheriff made his concluding statements, "And really to tell you the truth I trust you about as far as I can throw you."

"That's the first time someone has said that to me," replied Hound Dog.

"Well, I just need to spend more time with you. How about you come to church with us tomorrow morning and you, Tiffany, and I will have lunch together. Sound like a deal?"

"What about tonight?" asked Hound Dog.

"I'm sorry Maurice, but that's just not going to fly. I'll see you tomorrow morning for the 9:15 service on Main and Church Street," responded the sheriff.

"Alright, have a good night and I'll see you tomorrow." And Hound Dog proceeded to walk the gauntlet and say goodnight to the three musketeers in the living room.

After Hound Dog got in the car he said to Sasha, "Man, does he even know how long it took me to find a decent place to eat around here that is open after seven?"

Chapter 22- Well Done to Go

It was the second meeting with the "boss" in as many days. The three thugs were instructed to go to Chunky's Burger Boy at nine-thirty to have a special meeting. They were traveling in their non-descript Dodge Charger. Sparky and Trigger were in the backseat. The brains of the operation, Clayton, didn't trust their driving skills. And as you might have guessed by their nicknames they had fiery tempers and inclinations towards road rage. They had all done time together and were dead set on never going back to prison. But being thugs was all they knew how to do. Sparky and Trigger had disregarded the GED classes and the trade classes.

Clayton was reading the text message that the boss sent to him a couple of minutes earlier: "Go through the drive through and order three well-done Chunky Deluxe Meals with extra pickles, no lettuce, and no onions. For drinks make sure to get extra-large Muleshoe root beers. Look inside for the prize."

"What's it say, Clay?" asked Trigger, preferring to use Clayton's shortened name.

"It's a food order for Chunky's. Boss knows you guys like to eat, so he's taken care of you," answered Clayton.

The Dodge Charger approached the microphone for Clayton to place his order and a voice squawked over the speaker, "Welcome to Chunky's Burger Boy, Home of the Chunky-Monkey Burger, how may I help you?"

Clayton held up his cell phone so he could read off the order exactly, "I'll have three well-done Chunky Deluxe Meals with extra pickles, no lettuce and no onions."

Sparky interrupted from the back seat and whined, "No onions! But I like onions."

Clayton raised his hand for him to be quiet before completing the order by saying, "And all the drinks will be extra-large Muleshoe root beers."

The attendant answered back, "That will be $21.56, please pull around to the side to pay and pick up your meal."

Clayton drove up, glaring at Sparky in the rear-view mirror, "I don't care if you like onions or not, that's what the boss told us to order. Anyway, onions are somnific."

"Does that mean they are something terrific?" asked Sparky.

Rather than explain the real meaning Clayton conceded to just agree and said, "Yes, they are something terrific for you to ingest."

"What does ingest mean, Clay?" asked Trigger.

Clayton was starting to regret his choice of henchmen to assist him in his criminal exploits as he approached the window to pay and receive their order. He was formulating a snappy comeback to say to Trigger when he saw the attendant dressed in a flamboyant monkey suit at the window.

"Whoa, check out the guy at the window!" exclaimed Sparky as he started to roll down his window so he could poke fun at him.

"Enjoy your meal!" said the guy in the monkey suit, "And be sure to enjoy the prize in the bag."

Clayton then realized it was the boss in the monkey suit, but it was too late.

Sparky was already reaching out to tug on the monkey costume and saying something ridiculous, "Time to go back to the zoo!"

Clayton decided to steer the car clear while yelling, "Sparky! Sit back in your seat before I rip your arm off and beat you with it!"

"What's the matter, man? He just wanted to have some fun," said Trigger sticking up for his dim-witted friend.

"That guy in the monkey suit was the boss—he just handed us our next assignment!"

"Why doesn't he want us to know what he looks like?" asked Trigger.

"Because he doesn't trust criminals," answered Clay as they drove back to their apartment. They would eat and see what the boss had for them to do in the relative safety of their own home.

Then Sparky totally redeemed himself by asking, "But isn't the boss a criminal like us?"

Chapter 23- Dear Diary

Tiffany had watched Hound Dog leave her home that night from her upstairs window. She got a full report from her over-protective father and brothers. At least they hadn't chased him off like the other guys. She decided to write a journal entry to help her sort through all of her thoughts and emotions from the day.

July 20, 2012:

Today was quite a roller coaster of emotions. Had a nasty run-in with Cranky Larry from Hertsenville. Fortunately this really sweet guy, named Maurice, helped me and threw Larry out of the diner. Larry tried to mess up Maurice's car, but his big dog bit his hand. After that craziness, daddy came to the diner to make sure everything was okay and then ran off to go help someone else. Then after talking with Maurice for a little bit, he asked me out on a date. I couldn't believe it at first—I don't even know him. I told him he would have to talk to daddy first.

At dinner tonight daddy said that he was going to have to get to know him. He is so over-protective, but I know he loves me and doesn't want me to get hurt. This guy is different from all the rest. I can't quite put my finger on it, but I hope to figure it out. He is so mysterious. Daddy said he would invite him to come to church with us tomorrow. And after his conversation with daddy he said he would come tomorrow.

Maurice came over tonight to meet daddy and the brothers. I'm sure they threatened to tear him to pieces. And of course daddy chose to clean his gun at the dinner table—I'm sure that would've driven mommy crazy! I wish she was here so I could talk to her about life and love.

Chapter 24- New Assignment

Clayton, Trigger and Sparky arrived back at their apartment and dove in to their Chunky Deluxe Meals. It beat prison food by a mile, so they gratefully devoured their meals.

Sparky, talking with a mouthful of food said, "Whuts tha bos tay?"

Clayton didn't know whether to answer him or scold him, but he answered back, "When you're done chewing you can say that all over again."

Much to Clayton's chagrin, Trigger chimed in during his chowfest as well, "Ha said, 'Whuts tha bos say?'"

"You should have been a dentist, Trigger, but I still don't know what you guys are talking about," replied Clayton. His patience was wearing on him living with these two numbskulls, but good criminals were hard to find these days. Clayton knew that Trigger and Sparky were completely lost without him. They would end back in the slammer if he didn't keep them from doing hair-brained mistakes all the time.

All the while Clayton was thinking about them, Trigger and Sparky were carrying on a conversation with their mouths full of well-done burger and greasy fries. Maybe they assumed that they understood each other perfectly and kept talking simply by anticipating what the other would say in response to the other. Trigger could have been talking about the abundance of pickles on his burger and Sparky could have been talking about a water balloon. Clayton decided to leave them in their own world and start reading about their next assignment.

The letter inside read:

Tomorrow, two of you will go to Slick's Used Car Palace and Garage located at 73 Greystone Street. Hound Dog recently traded in his new car. Find out everything you can about the new car he's driving (title, registration, VIN#, year, make and model, etc.). I've included two detective badges inside for you to use at your discretion, and don't be afraid to play bad cop. Once you know something give me a call.

Clayton smiled to himself, and told the others, "Looks like we get to act like detectives tomorrow."

Chapter 25- Sunday Morning

Hound Dog couldn't remember the last time he had darkened the doorway of a church building. Maybe it was Sawtooth's funeral he thought to himself. Hound Dog was usually staying up too late on Saturday nights singing the Blues to make it to a Sunday morning service.

As he drove to the church Hound Dog wanted to listen to a little Blues to help him calm down, but he was out of range to receive WBLU. Sasha was in the backseat napping as usual, but Hound Dog insisted on talking to her, "Why am I so nervous? I can stand up in front of hundreds of people and sing. And now I am just going to be sitting next to the most beautiful woman in the world listening to someone else talking and I have crazy goose bumps and butterflies in my stomach. Is this what love feels like?"

Hound Dog peered over his shoulder to check on Sasha, and complained, "You're not even listening to me." Sasha put her paw over her ears to help block out the noise coming from the direction of the front seat.

When Hound Dog pulled into the church parking lot he saw Tiffany and her father standing by the front door waiting for him. Tiffany looked stunning; the sheriff looked stoic. Hound Dog parked the car under a shade tree and cracked the windows for Sasha to have some fresh air. "Be good girl," said Hound Dog to Sasha, "Don't eat the upholstery." And as Hound Dog approached the building he wondered to himself: *I wonder if there will be anyone here like me?*

"Good morning, Maurice," said the sheriff with an extended hand to shake.

"Good morning, sheriff; hello Tiffany," replied Hound Dog.

"Let's head on in and find a seat," said the sheriff.

As the trio made their way through the front doors, Hound Dog noticed the three horsemen of the apocalypse, Tiffany's brothers, waiting in the wings. Hound Dog gave them a nod and a hearty good morning.

For some reason the sheriff led the way all the way up to second pew—right up front. Hound Dog felt uncomfortable sitting all the way up there so close to the pulpit. The sheriff allowed Tiffany to go in first, and before Hound Dog could go into the pew to sit next to her the sheriff wedged himself between them and entered the pew.

Hound Dog thought to himself, *Aw, man! I was hoping to at least sit next to Tiffany.*

The service started soon after, so the three of them didn't have any awkward conversation about the weather or the elections coming up in November—Hound Dog was tired of that old conversation, anyway.

The service had a song and had a pause for announcements and time to meet people seated around them. Tiffany's brothers were actually seated right behind him, so he had another time to shake their hands again. Josiah about squeezed his hand off to emphasize his threat from the previous evening. Hound Dog reflected, *Man, he has a death grip. I would hate him to put that on my head like the old Van Macklenburg wrestling family.* He imagined Josiah crushing his temples as the next song began.

The worship band had a couple of guys that could play guitar, so Hound Dog watched them intently. But the words of the song quickened his mind. Words like healer, and mercy were the words that gripped him the most. And then the band started really rocking out—Hound Dog didn't know you could jack the volume that high in a church building. And Tiffany and the sheriff had their hands raised. *What kind of church is this?* thought Hound Dog.

Hound Dog's next question was, *Is this some type of show or do these people really believe in a God?* The sheriff's eyes were closed, and so was Tiffany's—they must know the words. When Hound Dog turned around to see Tiffany's brothers, he was surprised to see one of them crying and two of them seated. *Maybe Josiah is repenting for crushing my hand a few minutes ago*, thought Hound Dog.

The band switched gears and played an old hymn that Hound Dog remembered from his childhood, though he didn't know the name of it. Hound Dog was struck by the words as if he had never heard them before, "Prone to wander, Lord I feel it, prone to leave the God I love."[1]

Hound Dog felt like he had been running all his life.

---

[1] Robert Robinson, "Come, Thou Fount of Every Blessing," small portion of verse 3, 1758, alt.

Chapter 26- Slick's Second Interview

In Chicago, Slick was opening up his office when he noticed a black Dodge Charger driving into his car lot. Slick thought to himself, *Not the cops again, I've already talked with them before. I wonder what these guys want.*

Clayton had decided to bring Sparky on the condition that Sparky wore dark sunglasses and kept his mouth shut. Sparky was to follow Clayton's lead on when to show the detective's badge and when to break out the notebook and look busy. They had gone over the procedure at least five times in the car on the way over to Slick's car lot and garage; repetition is an excellent teacher.

Slick watched Clayton and Sparky get out of their car. They were dressed sharply, but the one wearing dark glasses was noticeably uncomfortable in the suit by the way he kept tugging at the lapels.

Clayton took the lead in opening the conversation, "We're looking for the proprietor of this business. I'm Detective Reynolds," presenting his badge, "and this is my partner, Detective Smith." Sparky took his cue and presented his badge quickly and nonchalantly. Clayton was pleased he didn't bungle the first step.

"I'm Slick, what do you need?" said Slick as he thought it odd that detectives were visiting him again. Hound Dog must be in some real trouble.

Clayton spoke quickly to try and sound official and in charge of the situation, "By court order we are going to need to requisition all of your sales records for the last week."

"What are you talking about? You can't just walk in here and take all of my sales records," replied Slick.

Clayton tried to smooth over his refusal with a more reasonable response, "Hey, I'm just doing my job; don't get mad at me."

"This is ridiculous! Let me see the court order."

Clayton smoothly pulled out a forged document from his sport jacket and showed it to Slick, "It's right here, plain and simple. And here's the judges signature."

Slick read over the document and kept up his protest, "I'm calling my lawyer," and proceeded to walk into his office.

Clayton and Sparky followed, and Clayton attempted to step-up his intimidation tactics, "Look, you don't want to go to jail for obstruction of justice—we know about your recent dealings with a wanted felon that goes by the nickname Hound Dog."

"So what?" quipped Slick.

"You don't want to go to jail for aiding and abetting a felon do you?" responded Clayton trying to sound official with all the legal terminology he could muster.

Slick had reached his desk, but before Slick could pick up his handset, Clayton yanked the phone cord out of the wall.

"Hey! What do you think you are doing!" yelled Slick.

Marshmallow sensed heightened danger and jumped off the desk and ran for the open door.

Sparky reacted aggressively to Slick's shouting and slammed Slick against the wall of his office. Slick's head hit the bottom shelf of his racing trophies and a number of them toppled on top of Slick. Then Sparky made the mistake of speaking, "Shut-up, we can do what we want to!"

Clayton tried to remind Sparky by yelling, "That's enough, Detective Smith!" But his admonition had little effect on Sparky. Clayton picked up the phone cord and wrapped it around Slick's ankles and wrists before Slick could recover from his collision with the back wall. Next, Clayton went to find any sales receipts or recent paperwork on Slick's messy desk.

Still in the tumult of his temper tantrum, Sparky forgot to use Clayton's false identity and misspoke, "Should I rough him up some more, Clayton?"

"No, you troglodyte, you've already done enough. Take this stack of receipts with you to the car," said Clayton.

Clayton then turned his attention to Slick who was crumpled on the floor struggling to free himself from his phone cord bonds and told him before swiftly exiting the office: "You're not going to say anything to anyone about what has happened here today; otherwise, we'll come back here and shut down your whole business."

Slick was not deterred in the least; he yelled back at him as he fought his bonds even harder than before, "You're lucky I'm all tied up right now! I would tear you limb from limb!"

Clayton and Sparky quickly drove off and left Slick all tied up. He would have to wait for Morris to show up later since it was a Sunday morning to be untied; the best Marshmallow could muster were frantic meows for not feeding her breakfast yet.

Still Slick retained his sense of humor through it all. He spoke to Marshmallow: "Any chance of you pulling off a 'Lassie' miracle by running to the kids around the block and telling them that I'm all tied up?" Then he thought to himself, *That wouldn't work.*

"I can see it now, Marshmallow," said Slick as he closed his eyes and imagined the whole rescue scene, "Look Bobby, it's Marshmallow. She's gyrating and making clicking noises—it must be Morse code. The message is: 'Man-servant is indisposed, I am starving. Please feed me!' Quick Bobby! Get some food for Marshmallow before she dies!"

Slick chuckled to himself; the comic relief helped him forget his bonds for a little while.

Chapter 27- Revelation

Back in Santiago, Hound Dog was listening intently to Pastor Eric's sermon on Jesus's miracle of turning water into wine. Hound Dog had the sensation that the pastor was talking to him directly, and it wasn't the fact that he was sitting on the second row. It really felt like the pastor had written the whole sermon for him to hear; almost as if no one else in the church needed to hear the same message.

The pastor was wrapping up his sermon and stared at Hound Dog as if they were holding a conversation and said, "Jesus is inviting you to the party of all parties, a celebration with the true master of ceremonies. Can you imagine sitting at a feast with Jesus?"

Hound Dog really wanted to answer the pastor's rhetorical question, but he caught himself. He looked around to see if the others in the church were tracking with the pastor as well as he was.

Pastor Eric continued, "The great news for us is that God wants us to spend eternity with Him in paradise. The problem we have as humanity is that none of us qualify for such an honor. Not even the most holy church lady, or the most devout follower of any faith. None of us, nobody, can reach the standard of perfection. So how can we answer Jesus' invitation?"

This question had bothered Hound Dog for a long time and was one of the reasons he didn't like going to church. He couldn't stand the actors that sang "Hallelujahs" on Sunday and then were slamming everybody for the remainder of the week. Hound Dog knew he wasn't perfect; in fact, he had made his fair share of mistakes. Instantly his mind shifted to the fight he had with the cops in the recording studio. Hound Dog cringed to think of it.

"You see, friends, this is where Jesus comes into the picture. His death on the cross paid the price for every person's wrongs. It's a free gift of undeserved mercy. Don't get me wrong, what we do here in this world counts for eternity, but it doesn't get you through the door," said the pastor from the pulpit. "We need to be people that seek to love people and make decisions that bless people as we walk daily with Jesus here on Earth."

Hound Dog had never heard about undeserved mercy before, he thought to himself, *I thought church was all about following rules and doing good so that God would love you and let you into heaven.*

And then the pastor spoke as if to answer Hound Dog's question: "This is the message of grace. We receive God's love as a gift, not by anything that we could do to attain perfection, but all by Jesus's death on the cross. This is why we celebrate Easter—the bodily resurrection proves that God the Father has accepted the sacrifice of Jesus. Friends, let's end with a song to praise the One that brings us true and lasting joy!"

With that pronouncement, the worship band fired up their guitars. Hound Dog hadn't even realized that the musicians had come back on stage. Everyone stood around Hound Dog, and Hound Dog reflexively stood up—he didn't want to stand out as the odd ball. The band was just as pumped up and loud as they were at the beginning. Hound Dog was already missing his regular guitar playing; maybe he could go up after the song and play a few bars.

When the service was over, Hound Dog told the sheriff and Tiffany that he was going to go to meet the guys in the band—musicians have a way of connecting that transcends creed and ego. As Hound Dog neared the top of the steps, the lead guitarist knew who he was: "Hey, I know who you are! You're Hound Dog. Thanks for joining us this morning. Do you want to jam this afternoon?"

Hound Dog was taken aback but who could pass up a chance to jam!

Chapter 28- Call out the Hounds

"Hey boss, I got good news for you," said Clayton as he sat in his apartment surrounded by Slick's paperwork strewn about the room.

"What's up?" answered the boss.

Holding up the title to the light to verify the information, Clayton proudly said, "You won't believe who is driving Kartow's Crown Vic?"

"Say it ain't so," in a much more excited tone.

"That's right, our *friend* Hound Dog is driving around with our mother-load of cocaine, and I bet he has no idea," said Clayton confidently.

"Excellent work; I want you to arrange for bounty hunters to track down Hound Dog, so we can get back what is rightfully ours."

Clayton was anticipating this request and asked: "What kind of cut will the hunters get when they bring in the catch?"

"Well, since we were expecting to pay for the whole thing, we can afford to split the stash 50-50 with them. That ought to give them greater impetus to find the quarry as well."

"I couldn't agree more," confirmed Clayton.

"Good, you make those arrangements and await further instructions," said the boss.

"Will do, boss man!" responded Clayton.

"Alright, I got to go; you stay out of trouble," and the boss clicked off.

"But trouble's my middle name," said Clayton laughing to himself.

Chapter 29- Chaperoned Lunch

After Hound Dog connected with the church band and worked out the details on their afternoon jam session, he drove over to Martha's Deli on Main Street to have lunch with Tiffany, and Sheriff Baker. The three of them sat crammed together at a small table in the corner; for some reason their table had a supporting column running right through the middle of it.

Hound Dog has trouble passing up on a Reuben Sandwich anytime he sees it on a menu, but soon after he was questioning his lunch choice. *What if the Thousand Island and sauerkraut get all over my face while I'm talking with Tiffany and her dad? That would be embarrassing.*

Tiffany's dad started off the conversation by asking Hound Dog, "Hound Dog, do you have any siblings?"

"I have two sisters that are much older than me. They are down south in Louisiana and Texas," answered Hound Dog.

"How was it having older sisters?" asked Tiffany curiously.

"It was great since they loved cooking, so they would make cookies and brownies some times; the rough part was scaring off all the boys that wanted to date my sisters," answered Hound Dog.

"Well, I guess you can understand how protective Tiffany's brothers are then, right?" responded Sheriff Baker.

Hound Dog nodded over to the three henchmen at their own little café table angled so they could keep an eye on Hound Dog, "Yeah, I understand their predicament."

"So how long have you been singing the Blues?" asked Tiffany.

"All my life; I used to get in to trouble in school and after a trip to see the principal I started singing about spankings. My classmates loved it and it consoled their own memories of being paddled."

The Sheriff interjected, "Yeah, you went to school in a different era when schools paddled kids; now they are too afraid of getting sued."

"Yeah, there was no mercy back in the day. Which reminds me of what the pastor was talking about today: what is this whole business about undeserved mercy?" inquired Hound Dog.

Tiffany spoke up, "In our human relationships and even our criminal justice system we don't see undeserved mercy. We see the wrong-doer punished."

"But to err is human, right?" asked Hound Dog.

"Moreover, we live in a broken and hurting world. I'm sure you are acquainted with that in singing the Blues," said the Sheriff.

"But why did God make a world all messed up like this?" asked Hound Dog.

Tiffany, thought she had a good answer so she said, "You see Hound Dog, God created a perfect world, but He also created us with a free will to choose whether to follow Him or not. And when Adam and Eve disobeyed God the world was no longer perfect. That is why we see a broken creation and broken human relationships."

"Why didn't God just grant them undeserved mercy at that moment?" asked Hound Dog.

Tiffany answered honestly, "I don't know, but I think He had a long-term solution in sending His Son, Jesus, into this cursed world to rescue mankind. He didn't leave us."

Hound Dog was grateful that the food was being delivered to the table, for one he was famished, and two he was getting uncomfortable talking about religion with Tiffany and Sheriff Baker. In hopes of changing the subject Hound Dog said, "Oh look, the food is here."

After the food was served, the Sheriff caught Hound Dog right as he was going to grab his succulent Reuben sandwich and asked, "Maurice, do you mind if we pray for the meal?"

"Oh, certainly go right ahead," replied Hound Dog. Internally he was thinking to himself, *Strike two! Caught trying to eat my sandwich before praying!*

The Sheriff nodded to Tiffany and she prayed, "Heavenly Father, thank you for a beautiful day and the freedom to worship you. Thank you for Hound Dog's life and how you have created him with special skills and talents. We ask for your blessing upon this food that you provided for us. In Your Holy name, Amen."

After the prayer was over, Hound Dog couldn't help but asking, "What would happen if you didn't pray for the meal before eating?"

Tiffany explained with a straight face, "The food would rot in our stomachs, and we would die a very long and painful death," and then she smiled to let him know she was joking.

Chapter 30- Calling All Thugs

Clayton was driving to see a gang leader and was reflecting on their lucky find. At first the boss thought it would be nice to know where to point the detectives, but now there was the potential bonus of recovering the drug stash Kartow stole from them.

He arrived at a hole-in-the-wall bar called, The Unlucky where a group called "The Cannibals" hung out. If they couldn't find Hound Dog, no one could.

Clayton found the leader of The Cannibals, Jupiter Links, at the back of the bar. He had the gang's signature tattoo on his neck: a skeleton sitting in a big black boiling cauldron. Clayton cringed seeing it because getting a tattoo on your neck has got to be painful.

Jupiter Links knew what Clayton wanted and told him, "Take a seat; let's talk business."

Clayton was straight to the point, "I'm looking for a Blues singer named Hound Dog; he is sitting on a stash of cocaine worth a couple of million dollars. You interested?"

"When was this guy last seen?" asked Jupiter.

"Friday morning he got in a fight with some cops, and took off," answered Clayton.

Jupiter fired off another question, "What did he do?"

"He robbed a bank."

"What's that got to do with the cocaine?" inquired Jupiter.

"Have you heard of a dead, crooked cop named, Kartow? Hound Dog was working with him and he is driving his car with the stash." answered Clayton.

Jupiter's eyes narrowed and he said, "I knew who Kartow was, but how come I haven't heard of this guy, Hound Dog?"

Clayton had to think of some more lies to cover up his previous lies, and decided to focus on the known enemy, "You know Kartow; he had his dirty, little, grubby hands in all sorts of places."

"So what's in it for us?" asked Jupiter.

"You can keep 25% of the stash, and do whatever you like with it," answered Clayton, knowing that he would tell the boss he had split it 50-50 with the bounty hunters.

"What about this Hound Dog character? What do you want us to do with him?" asked Jupiter, as he was already thinking what he was going to do with the *entire* stash of coke. Greed works wonders.

"You just worry about getting the drugs; I don't care what happens to him. He has enough trouble with the law after him," replied Clayton. He then handed over the Crown Victoria's paperwork to Jupiter. "He's driving Kartow's old Crown Vic. You find the car, and bring it back for us to divvy up the loot."

Jupiter stuck out his hand for the two criminals to shake on the agreement and said, "Pleasure doing business with you, and here's my card. Call my cell if you have any more information on this Hound Dog character. In the meantime, I will put out my feelers."

Chapter 31- A Chance to Jam

After lunch with Tiffany and her dad, Hound Dog went back up to the church to play guitar with the church band. Fortunately, he had his American Special Fender Stratocaster in the trunk and he didn't have to go back to the motel to pick it up. Sasha had already been on her stroll, so she was set to relax in the car for a Sunday afternoon nap with the car windows down.

He met Larson and Louis in the sanctuary, and started getting plugged in and ready to rock. After two fights in three days Hound Dog needed to blow off some steam by playing his guitar. But before they got started Hound Dog asked an off-the-cuff question, "So how much do you get paid for playing on Sunday mornings?" He was trying to see if it would be way to earn some money while in Santiago.

"We don't get paid, we just volunteer as a way to serve in the church," answered Larson.

"That's a bummer," answered Hound Dog thinking more about himself not being able to get some income if he also started playing on Sunday mornings.

Louis invited Hound Dog to lead off and said they would follow along, so Hound Dog let rip some of his favorite Blues riffs. It felt good to play again, and he enjoyed the acoustics of the sanctuary. Hound Dog's fingers felt at home once again.

Chapter 32- Man-to-Man Talk

After the jam session at the church, Hound Dog felt that he needed to talk with the Sheriff about what was going on in his life. His heart and mind felt divided; part of him was saying to run out of fear and part of him was saying to stay and pursue love. Hound Dog recognized that Sheriff Baker was a man that he could trust. He might end up spending the night in jail, but Hound Dog knew he had to level with the sheriff.

Hound Dog knocked on the Baker's front door, and the sheriff answered the door and said, "Hey Hound Dog, Tiffany is out with her brothers. I'm sure you could go find them at the park around the corner."

"Well, you know I actually was looking to talk with you about some things," replied Hound Dog.

"Sure, come on in," said the sheriff.

Hound Dog was sensing that the sheriff was warming up to him, and he thought to himself, *Now I am going to mess everything up when I tell him I am a wanted felon.*

"So, what's on your mind?" asked Sheriff Baker.

"Well, to tell you the truth a lot of things are going on," said Hound Dog, "I really don't know where to start."

"Don't worry, nothing you say will be held against you in a court of law," said the sheriff with a chuckle.

Hound Dog laughed uncomfortably and played up the joke, "Maybe I should request a lawyer." And they had some more awkward laughter between them before Hound Dog said, "But seriously, I am here to talk about something that happened in Chicago."

Sheriff Baker's demeanor changed and his head cocked to the side so he could get a better look at Hound Dog, "What are you talking about, Hound Dog?"

Hound Dog decided to lay it all out, "I beat up three cops on Friday morning in Chicago."

"What?" asked the sheriff, "Give me the whole story; you are skipping to the chase."

"Okay, let me back up," Hound took a deep breath and continued, "We just started recording a new album in the Tri-City recording studio, and we were really jamming. It was awesome, but then three cops busted out of the wall and started shouting and telling us to stop. When lead cop stuffed a pepper mace can in my face I flew off the handle. I hit him a couple of times with my guitar and knocked out the other two cops that were with him. Then I split like nobody's business."

The sheriff's hand went up to grip his mouth as if he couldn't believe his ears. An attack on his fellow law enforcement colleagues was hitting a nerve, but he was holding it in. The sheriff asked Hound Dog to keep talking.

"So I took off, I bought an old cop car and I even bought a fake driver's license and social security card."

The sheriff's eyes got bigger and his other hand swept across his mouth. Hound Dog thought the sheriff was about to fall out of his chair and imagined what the sheriff was thinking, *A criminal in my own home with the audacity to try steal my daughter. Where are my handcuffs?*

The sheriff only said, "Continue."

"I hit the road and had a flat tire, this is when I discovered that my trunk had a huge cache of cocaine bricks," said Hound Dog, and this was when the sheriff's eyebrows shot toward the ceiling and his eyes bugged out like a madman. Hound Dog continued talking, "And then I came into Santiago and fell in love with an angel named Tiffany."

"Anything else you want to tell me?" asked Sheriff Baker half wondering if anything crazier could be mentioned.

"Maybe the strangest thing happened today," started Hound Dog, "I went to a church where people were raising their hands and singing. And I heard about this thing called 'undeserved mercy.'"

"Let me ask you a question, Hound Dog," interjected the sheriff, "What kind of relationship did you have with your dad?"

Hound Dog had rehearsed what he was going to say, but in all truth he really wasn't ready for that type of question. Hound Dog cocked his neck back to think for a moment before saying, "My father wasn't around much. And when he was around he was strict like all get out."

"Did your dad ever tell you he loved you?" asked the sheriff.

"No," answered Hound Dog bluntly.

"Did your dad ever tell you he was proud of you?"

"No, he didn't. But I wish like the dickens he had," answered Hound Dog.

"Well, Hound Dog," said Sheriff Baker with a pause, "I am going to tell you I am proud of you for coming to me to tell me about all of these things going on in your life. I know you are a fighter and I like that about you. But you are going to have to face these problems before you can pursue a relationship with my daughter."

"What do you mean?" asked Hound Dog.

"Do you have someone in Chicago you trust? Someone who can help you face these criminal charges?" asked the sheriff.

"I think so, the guys at Tri-City have always gone to bat for me," answered Hound Dog.

Chapter 33- Calling Home

When Hound Dog got back to the Stardust Motel he was determined to set things right back in Chicago and not run away from his problems anymore. He knew the guys at Tri-City would be there for him. Hound Dog dialed Tri-City to see if anyone was at the head office on Sunday night. Surprisingly, someone picked up the phone.

Hound Dog was caught off guard and said, "Hey, Lightning, is that you?"

"Hound Dog?" answered Lightning Watkins.

"Yes, it's me."

"Where are you? We've been worried sick about you. Are you doing okay?" asked Lightning in quick succession.

"Yeah, I'm alright. I'm in Santiago, Indiana. I've met some people who have helped me out and are helping me face my legal problems," confessed Hound Dog.

"Wow, that's great man. I'm so happy to hear that you're safe. Do you need someone to come pick you up?" asked Lightning.

"No, I have a car and I'll be coming back to Chicago to settle everything and face the criminal charges," replied Hound Dog.

"Where can I reach you in case I need to get in touch with you? And we'll help you walk through this. You know you can trust us," reassured Lightning Watkins.

"I'm at the Stardust Motel here in Santiago," answered Hound Dog.

"Oh, good, I see it on the phone—I'll take down the number," said Lightning.

"Good, I'll see you later. Maybe you can come visit me in the county jail," said Hound Dog with a laugh, "Guess I can always get some more Blues material there."

Lightning responded, "Okay, you know you've always been able to see the positive in every situation. You hang in there."

Chapter 34- What's a Girl to Do?

Tiffany Baker was having another rough night as her mind was racing through the events of the day. She was wrestling with her thoughts and questions about Hound Dog, and finally decided to write all of them out in her journal so she could put them on paper and out of her mind.

Why am I thinking so much about a person I barely know?

Where did he come from?

Why now?

What would his sisters say about him?

Could I really see myself marrying him in the future?

Do I want to marry a Blues musician?

Why I am thinking about marriage?

Will I ever get married?

Does Maurice even want to get married?

Why am I still thinking about Maurice?

Would I be Mrs. Hound Dog?

Ugh!! I'm going back to bed!

Chapter 35- Head Hunters Biker Gang

Once Jupiter got word from Clayton that Hound Dog was staying at the Stardust Motel in Santiago, Indiana he sent a two-man team on a single Harley Davidson to pull off a simple operation: Jupiter's best car thief, Clutch, and his best motorcycle driver, Shark, were going to ride down to Santiago, hotwire the car and bring it back to Chicago. What could go wrong?

Both Shark and Clutch had the signature Head-Hunters tattoo on their necks: a skeleton boiling in a black cauldron. It was a mark they bore proudly because it commanded respect. For esteem and a sense of belonging are what all gang members really long to attain.

After they located the Stardust Motel they laid waiting in the vacant lot across the state highway for Hound Dog's Crown Victoria to come back to the motel. They recognized the temporary paper license plate that was issued by Slick's Used Car Palace and Garage. But Shark and Clutch weren't the only one waiting for Hound Dog and Sasha to get back for the night. Larry from Saturday morning had taken care of his broken hand and was determined to exact his revenge on Hound Dog.

After Hound Dog and Sasha arrived back and settled down for the night, Larry's pick-up truck rolled slowly behind the former cop car and came to a stop. Larry got out of the truck and walked around to the Crown Victoria.

Larry's pick-up blocked Clutch and Shark's view of the Crown Victoria.

"Who's that? And what's he doing?" asked Clutch.

"Your guess is as good as mine," answered Shark, "Let's just wait and see."

Clutch nervously asked, "Do you think he is after the coke as well?"

"I don't think so," and motioned Clutch to be quiet, "Listen, what's that hissing sound."

"Look, he's getting back in the truck," said Shark, "let's go see what he did."

Clutch and Shark walked nonchalantly over to see the Crown Victoria in the motel parking lot, but were surprised to see that all four tires had been slashed.

Clutch knew this was a bad sign and called Jupiter's cell phone immediately.

Jupiter answered the phone, "What's up? You on your way back, yet?"

Clutch hated reporting bad news to the boss, and cringing as he said, "One of the local yokels just ripped up all of the car's tires—we are going to need a tow truck."

Jupiter was to the point, "Hold tight; we'll be there in two hours."

Chapter 36- Sunday Night Calling

The dreaded phone call had come once again. He really didn't want to answer his cell phone, but he had to do it.

"Hello."

"I told you I would call to see how you are progressing with returning my stuff; do you have anything to report?"

"We are making some headway, and we are hopeful to give you a large chunk of your stuff back, and we will pay you for the remaining portion."

"Excellent. That's what I like to hear. I'll give you a call on Tuesday to arrange the payment and return details. And don't get any silly ideas and try something on me."

"I've got a good crew; they won't try to cross you."

"Good, I hope they live up to your estimation." And with those final words he cut off the call abruptly.

Chapter 37- Jupiter to the Rescue

When Jupiter came with his Ford F650 Super Duty wrecker its diesel engine was knocking so loud you would think it would wake up most of the Stardust Motel. Fortunately there weren't that many people in the motel and it was already past two in the morning.

Hound Dog knew what was happening, and Sasha started to bark.

"Be quiet, Sasha," said Hound Dog assuring the wolf that everything was alright.

Hound Dog heard the distinctive lock and load of some type of firearm right outside his door. These guys weren't messing around. Hound Dog thought to himself, *If these guys want my car that bad, they can have it!* He recognized the car thieves' distinctive Chicago accents.

Since Larry slashed all the tires it took a while to get the dolly carriage under the front wheels, but lifting the back was completed faster than a forklift. They had no need to be careful; they just wanted the goods locked inside. Clutch and Shark manned the door where they had seen Hound Dog go inside, room number 14. They both had shotguns at the ready if Hound Dog tried to stop them.

Hound Dog crawled out of the bed and brought the phone down on the floor. He called the sheriff to let him know what was happening, "The fish have taken the bait and they're getting ready to drag it back to Chicago with a wrecker."

The sheriff gave Hound Dog instructions, "Stay inside, and don't make any noises. I'll come and pick you up in the morning. Over and out."

Fortunately, the sheriff had anticipated trouble when Hound Dog had mentioned the giant load of cocaine sitting in the back of his trunk. Sheriff Baker had decided it would be prudent for Hound Dog to voluntarily impound the car he bought from Slick. Sheriff Baker's plan was working out perfectly as the replacement black Crown Victoria was readily accepted as Kartow's former cop car. To catch the thieves he had to catch them in the act of stealing the car, so he had to be patient.

Jupiter gave the signal to Clutch and Shark to get ready to go. "Get in the cab, Clutch. Shark, you follow the truck and try and keep up." Jupiter hopped in the cab of his truck, and rolled abruptly out of the parking lot with the Crown Victoria in tow.

The wrecker was roaring down the road and Jupiter was already engrossed in calculating the amount of money he would get from selling the cocaine on the streets of Chicago. He felt like Candide did when he had all those large sheep loaded with gold nuggets. But Jupiter was counting his proverbial chickens before they hatched. He had only been on the road a couple of minutes when Jupiter saw police lights flashing in his rear view mirror. His instincts took over and he pressed the accelerator harder. Next, he rolled his window down and gave Shark a thumb down signal.

Shark knew his job was to take out the police car and give Jupiter time to get away. He slowed down just a hair and pulled a 180 degree turn so that he was now facing the pursuing police car that was in hot pursuit. Shark readied his shotgun and fired buckshot rapidly at the car. The police car's front tires blew out and Deputy Henricks hit the brakes to skid to a halt. Within seconds he was on the radio, "Shots fired! I repeat; shots fired! My car is out of commission."

Sheriff Baker's plan was coming together, but it had taken a dangerous turn. These criminals were serious and were escalating the confrontation more than he expected.

"Henricks, take evasive action!" ordered Sheriff Baker. He didn't want to see anyone get hurt, especially one of his men. Henricks had volunteered for the task of pushing the thieves into the sheriff's trap, and he done it well; yet, it wasn't worth getting killed over.

Deputy Henricks climbed over his computer console and made his way out of the passenger side door. He could hear the armed motorcyclist coming towards him on his bike, so he ran for cover and had his sidearm at the ready. Shark sped by the vehicle and fired three more times into the vehicle before turning sharply to chase after Jupiter's wrecker.

Henricks radioed the sheriff, "Sheriff, I'm safe. Motorcyclist is chasing after the wrecker and coming your way!"

Chapter 38- The Trap Springs Eternal

"Deputies and troopers, we have suspects that are armed and dangerous. Exercise extreme caution," radioed the sheriff to his cohort situated on a hundred feet of narrow road under a rail bridge. The wrecker would have nowhere to run.

The sheriff went to his trunk and readied his assault rifle. He was a crack shot and would give the order to take out the wrecker's tires and engine block. The sheriff didn't want to risk the truck trying to ram through the vehicles. The night was quiet, but soon he could hear the loud clatter of the diesel engine racing towards him.

Jupiter was racing around the corner as fast as he could, and was shocked to see a whole contingent of cop cars waiting for him as he sped downwards under the railway. He yelled for Clutch to get his shotgun ready, and raced at the roadblock.

"On my order take out the wrecker's engine and tires… FIRE!" yelled the sheriff.

Jupiter saw the muzzle flashes and then he heard the quick popping sounds of gunfire.

Clutch yelled out, "There shooting at us!" and instinctively ducked from the window.

Jupiter swerved the large wrecker to dodge the bullets, but that was an impossible proposition. The wrecker rammed into the retaining wall. The airbags deployed and saved Jupiter and Clutch's lives. Neither one was wearing their seatbelts, so they were slammed around like ragdolls in a washing machine. And before they could regain themselves they were surrounded by law enforcement and wearing handcuffs behind their backs. The thieves were fortunate they weren't dead.

Within one minute came Shark, racing full speed with his shotgun ready for action. As he neared the roadblock he fired off his shotgun indiscriminately in the direction of lawmen.

"Shots fired, shots fired," yelled the deputies as they scattered from the truck's mangled carcass.

The sheriff measured a single shot to take out Shark's front tire and caused the bike's front end to decelerate instantaneously. Shark was thrown off the front of the bike as the rear end swung quickly up into the air like a catapult. Miraculously he survived the crash and was taken to the county hospital under custody.

Chapter 39- Where is He?

It was the early hours of Monday morning and Clayton was visibly upset and his mind was racing through all of the possible scenarios of failure. His conclusion was that Jupiter had crossed him and taken the drugs for himself.

"How could I be so stupid to trust Jupiter and his group of cannibals to bring the stash back to us?"

Clayton was talking out loud to himself primarily and this monologue allowed Trigger and Sparky to keep abreast of the situation, "Jupiter isn't answering his phone and he isn't responding to any of my texts."

Sparky thought he could encourage Clayton by saying, "Jupiter is probably asleep. Why don't you just call him around lunch time."

Clayton was more cynical, "There's no way he's going to be sleeping while sitting on a small fortune. He's probably on his way to make a big sale in Detroit by now."

Trigger was more reflective, "I'm telling you, man, this load of coke is cursed. First it was picked up by that crooked cop and he tried to extort us with it, and then it gets taken by a two-bit Blues singer, and now another crook gets his hands on it. I'm telling you it's cursed."

Clayton was starting to believe it was cursed as well, "The boss isn't going to be happy when he has to pay Canton for this rotten stash of drugs," pounding his fist to release some of his anger, "that's going to be the lion's share of the bank job."

Chapter 40- Jupiter Wants His Lawyer

On Monday morning Jupiter and Clutch found themselves in separate jail cells. They were covered from head to toe with bandages and band aids. Jupiter had a headache that rivaled his worst hangover. After a simple breakfast at 6 am the sheriff came to visit Jupiter's cell and escort him to the interrogation room.

"Good morning, Mr. Jones," said Sheriff Baker.

Jupiter squinted and faintly remembered that the fake Illinois driver's license was "Tecumseh Sherman Jones". Evidently he also got his driver's license from Fredrico's Tamale Hut—the historic twist was a dead giveaway.

"What is your date of birth?" asked the sheriff.

"I want my lawyer," answered Jupiter.

With a smile the sheriff responded, "No problem, here's the phone."

Jupiter lifted the phone and called his brother Marvin in Chicago, "Hey, Marvin. It's me. I'm in jail in Santiago, Indiana; can you get my lawyer for me?"

Jupiter just cringed. Evidently Marvin didn't get along with Jupiter because he slammed the phone down without a word. The sound reverberated through his brain and he winced with pain.

The sheriff was hopeful to get the phone number traced so he could start gaining some information on Jupiter.

"So what's with the matching tattoos you three guys all have?" asked the sheriff.

"I want my lawyer," responded Jupiter plainly.

Chapter 41- Picking Up the Pieces

Sheriff Baker came by to pick up Hound Dog and Sasha shortly after 8 am at the Stardust Motel and took them over to Breakfast at Tiffany's. Hound Dog was wondering what happened last night, but he was reticent to ask. Hound Dog thought to himself, *Maybe the bad guys got away, or maybe someone got hurt.*

Instead of asking, he made small talk, "Nice weather we're having don't you think?"

"Yeah, it's been nice lately," responded the sheriff.

Then there was awkward silence for the remaining minute or two as they drove to the diner. It wasn't until they parked the car that Sheriff Baker said, "You did well, Hound Dog. You kept quiet and didn't do anything stupid last night. The guys we caught were armed and dangerous."

"Are all of your deputies alright?" asked Hound Dog.

"I don't like to revel in these types of matters, but I will tell you no one was killed, and the criminals are all alive as well," answered the sheriff.

Hound Dog gulped and said, "Thanks sheriff for telling me what to do when the thieves came for the car."

"It looks like they had tabs on where to find you," responded the Sheriff Baker.

"Lightning Watkins must have told somebody I was in Santiago," said Hound Dog.

"These criminals have a lot of ways to get information out of people and ways to listen in on peoples' phone calls—it's pretty scary what they can do these days. Especially when you're dealing with large sums of cash," explained the sheriff.

"That's wild," responded Hound Dog.

"Speaking of phone numbers, there is a phone number in here that has been trying to reach one of the criminals from last night; at least six text messages and a good number of missed calls," said the sheriff as he handed Hound Dog a thick envelope, "It's a Chicago number and I put in some technical details of the phone here in our custody; the authorities in Chicago will know what to do to find out who is calling, and how this person is connected to these thieves."

Their conversation was interrupted by a radio blurb, "*Screech*, 16-22, I got a situation at the jail with one of last night's perpetrators; report back to the jail; over."

The sheriff responded back into his radio, "Base, this is 16-22. I'm on my way; over and out."

"Hound Dog, it looks like I gotta' roll; I'll be praying for you as you go back to take care of things in Chicago; please read the letter before you go to the police station," said the sheriff in his earnest manner.

After Hound Dog got Sasha out of the back seat, he said to the sheriff through the open passenger door, "Thanks sheriff for showing me undeserved mercy."

"My pleasure; I'm just passing on a little bit of what's been given to me."

Chapter 42- This is for the Chiefs

Hound Dog tied up Sasha outside under a small shade tree and went inside of Breakfast at Tiffany's. He was glad for the opportunity to see her again and thought to himself, *She really is the most beautiful woman on the planet. Just look at how she treats people with kindness and respect.*

"Hello, Maurice," she said when she was done helping some customers.

"Thanks a ton for letting me borrow your car; I promise I'll keep Sasha from eating the seats and floor mats," said Hound Dog.

"Don't worry about it," she said with a laugh, "Daddy is going to pick me up and take me home after the lunch clean-up; I have a good feeling that this is all going to work out and you can bring it back to me in person," Tiffany said with an optimistic lilt in her voice.

"I'll keep it parked in a garage, so if anything happens you'll know where you can pick it up," assured Hound Dog, "and here is a note I want you to read after I've hit the road."

"Okay, I'll save it for later," she said and she carefully put it in her apron.

"Well, Tiffany, I've got to get on the road if I want to make it there by lunch time," said Hound Dog.

"Here are the car keys, and I gassed it up this morning," she said with a smile, "Oh and by the way, here's a small letter I want you to read later today when you need some encouragement." The letter smelled sweet like fruity perfume, and Hound Dog put it in his coat pocket.

"It looks like the Baker Clan is full of letter writers; I think I'd fit in well with you guys," said Hound Dog.

"Well, you just take care of business in Chicago and come back to see us," said Tiffany.

Hound Dog thought to himself, *What a woman!* Hound Dog held up his fist for a fist-bump with the woman of his dreams, and told her, "Don't tell your brothers I touched you."

She just laughed, but Hound Dog was dead serious. Hound Dog's chest hadn't felt the same since Josiah hugged him.

Chapter 43- Message in an Apron

Tiffany couldn't wait to read the letter that Hound Dog wrote to her. After the breakfast rush was finished, she sat in a booth with a nice cup of tea and read the letter slowly.

My Dearest Tiffany,

Being a songwriter I feel that it is easier for me to express my heart when I write my words down. Better yet I would be able to sing these words to you, but this letter will have to suffice.

My world has been rocked since meeting you—in a good way of course! I sure am glad I stopped in here for breakfast on Saturday morning. I've never met a woman as beautiful as you. You are a knock-out, but you are even more beautiful on the inside.

You and your dad have given me courage to face the problems that I created for myself back in Chicago. And hopefully I am a better man for that already. I've been running away from my problems for too long.

I really do hope things work out for me to come back to Santiago to pursue a relationship with you. But if things go sour I want you to know where your car will be parked. I made a map for you with the address on the next page.

Thanks for being a true friend.

Sincerely,
Hound Dog

Chapter 44- Back to Chicago

For Hound Dog the hardest part of getting back to Chicago was determining if Tiffany's Toyota Prius was actually on or not. Hound Dog thought to himself, *Sounds like the fan is spinning, but what about the engine?* But as soon as he engaged drive the little puppy was off and he actually enjoyed the low amount of engine noise. It allowed him to listen to his music more easily. And before he knew it he was within radio range of WBLU 108.1 FM. It had been too long since he had enjoyed some good Chicago Blues; Sasha just covered her ears. It was one of Hound Dog's favorite groups, Slim Walker and the Mudcats, and they were singing their classic hit, "Levy Done Broke".

> *The storm raged up river, like never before,*
> *And the heavens opened up something nasty.*
> *The levy was tested and found strong,*
> *But come midnight the levy was done.*
>
> *The fury of the river, like never before,*
> *Came rushing down upon us awful.*
> *The house was swamped and soaked to the bone,*
> *But come morning the house was gone.*
>
> *The river sat stagnant, like never before,*
> *And we floated till we were out of harm.*
> *The levy was tested and found wanting,*
> *And now the levy was no more.*

Chapter 45- Barking Up the Wrong Tree

Detectives Fortnight and Cole were having an average Monday morning. The 9 am precinct meeting with the "blow dryer" didn't go too well, but that was par for the course. After a couple of hours of shuffling paperwork the detectives made a short stop at the local coffee shop before they were on their way to 7th Heaven Guitar Shop on Oldham and West 7th Street. Detective Fortnight had tracked down Hound Dog's favorite guitar shop owned by Mike Johnson. The detectives were talking in the car.

"Man, the chief was so hot he almost had a conniption fit this morning," said Cole.

"Yeah, something about a big shootout that happened in northern Indiana last night," responded Fortnight.

"Like that has anything to do with us in Chicago," scoffed Cole.

"Here's the guitar place; let's see what we can find out about our main man, Hound Dog," said Fortnight.

Upon entering the store the detectives went straight back to Mike Johnson's office to ask him some questions. The detectives were completely ignorant of the quality and depth that the store possessed. In addition, the store's walls were covered with autographed pictures of all the greats that had purchased the guitars at 7th Heaven. The detectives were focused on finding their man.

Cole was straight to the point, "Mr. Johnson, I'm Detective Cole, and this is my partner Detective Fortnight. Do you mind if we ask you a few questions?"

"Sure, I don't have any customers right now, so I'm free to help you," answered Mike in a relaxed manner.

"Do you recognize this man?" asked Fortnight holding up a picture of Hound Dog.

"Sure I do, that's Hound Dog; he plays a wicked American Special Fender Stratocaster," answered Mike.

"When was the last time you saw Hound Dog?" asked Cole.

"Oh, 'bout a couple weeks ago," he replied casually.

"What was the nature of his visit?" asked Cole.

"Let me see," thinking to himself, "he came in to buy some strings and a vacuum tube," Mike answered proudly that he remembered a detail from a couple of weeks ago.

"Does Hound Dog have any large debts with you or anyone else you know?" asked Fortnight.

"No, I don't sell anything on credit, 'IOU', or 'I'll pay you on my next payday,'" answered Mike emphatically. The detectives had hit a nerve. Mike was just getting started on his soapbox, "I tell my customers: this isn't a pawn shop, and I am *not* a bank. I take all the major credit cards listed on the door, but I don't give loans."

"Alright," said Cole trying to draw the conversation back in.

But Mike was determined to have his say, and he continued on with his monologue, "No customer walks out of here with my merchandise without paying for it in full. You hear me? I've got some guitars in here that are worth more than your average used car. These are finely tuned instruments," and shaking his head for emphasis, "and they are NOT free!"

"Yes," said Fortnight to break off the discourse, "thank you for your time. We're going to be going now, but here are our calling cards. Please call us if you see Hound Dog."

And the detectives exited 7th Heaven Guitar Shop and went outside to get back in their car.

"We really need a break through, anything. How could this guy just vanish into thin air?" complained Fortnight.

"Be patient young *padawan*; you must use the force," said Cole in his best Obi-Wan voice before laughing at his own joke.

But the humor was lost on Fortnight and he responded, "Yeah, we'll see how much you'll be laughing when the chief fires us for incompetency."

Chapter 46- Facing the Facts

Hound Dog parked the car in a long-term parking garage that was close to the local dog salon, Dog Curler of Seville. He figured that if he wasn't able to get out of jail on bond they would take care of Sasha for him. Hound Dog hadn't completely worked out the details but he hoped Tiffany could pick up Sasha when she came to pick up her car.

Now it was time for Hound Dog to take care of business. He remembered the sheriff's letter in the thick envelope and was curious what the sheriff would say to him at this junction in time—Hound Dog felt like they left on good terms this morning. *I hope he doesn't say that he doesn't want to ever see me in the state of Indiana again. Or maybe it is a restraining order*

This is what the letter said:

Dear Maurice "Hound Dog" Jackson,

I hope these thoughts encourage you and sustain you for the coming challenge.

It is no accident that our paths crossed. I know my lovely daughter played a part as well, but I know it all happened for a reason. You needed someone who would challenge you to accept responsibility for what you had done in Chicago, and you have responded admirably. A real man will own up to his failings and quit running from them.

I want you to know that whatever happens with your case; I will be on your side. Whether that means jail or prison time, or come what may; I will not give up on you.

Many a man has come out of prison a better man than when he went in to the system. It was the decisions they made to use the time of suffering and breaking as a crucible to refine them for life after prison.

Sincerely,

Sheriff Baker

Hound Dog took courage from those reassuring words and walked the longest mile of his life to the 9th Precinct to turn himself in to the police. Going up the precinct steps was the hardest part. Hound Dog felt like each foot weighed three hundred pounds as he took each calculated step up the stairs. He thought to himself, *Love is a really strange motivator; I can't believe I am really doing this.*

Hound Dog walked up to the glass enclosed desk at the front, and spoke through a metal disc with slits punched out, "I'm here to confess beating up three cops last Friday morning."

The sergeant behind the desk was incredulous and asked, "What did you say?" The sound blaring through a cheap speaker attached to the ceiling.

"I said, 'I'm here to confess beating up three cops last Friday morning,'" said Hound Dog thinking that the metal disc was still blocking his confession.

"What are you talking about? Three cops weren't beaten up last Friday," answered the sergeant.

"What?" asked Hound Dog in a stunned manner.

"Look, if it happened I would know about it," answering proudly, "Now if you will excuse me I've got to go get a bite to eat. But take it from me—you better keep off the hard stuff," said the sergeant as he got up from his desk and walked away from his post behind the glass.

Hound Dog couldn't believe his ears; this didn't make any sense at all. He cautiously turned and started to walk out of the precinct lobby half-expecting the police to pounce on him. But then Hound Dog noticed a bulletin board covered with wanted posters, and one of them caught his attention immediately—it was his own silly looking Illinois driver's license photo from eight years ago. *No wonder the sergeant didn't even have a clue that I was the same guy on the wanted poster.*

Hound Dog quickly looked around to see that no one would see him take his own wanted poster off the wall with his best ninja swipe. He wanted to read it outside the station when no one else was looking. Hound Dog thought to himself, *Wouldn't I look like an imbecile standing there reading my own wanted poster?*

Chapter 47- Connection Established

Hound Dog could not believe his eyes when he read over his wanted poster on the street. He read the wanted poster out loud so his own ears could hear the news, "This is unreal: 'Mr. Jackson is suspected of masterminding the plot to steal four million dollars from the 3rd National Bank of Chicago. The fugitive is considered armed and dangerous. Exercise extreme caution when arresting him.'"

"I can't believe this! I've been framed for a bank heist! This is even worse than before."

At that moment Hound Dog didn't know where to turn. He needed an ally. It looked like things were turning worse than he had expected. Hound Dog started processing his next immediate steps, *I'm going to take Tiffany's car to the parking lot behind my apartment building and try and get out of this mess. Plus, I am going to get Sasha out of the beauty salon. Hopefully she hasn't eaten any of the other dogs.*

On his drive to his apartment, his mind was racing with all of the choices that lay in front of him. This time he called out to God, "God, what am I going to do? I tried to confess to the crime I know I did, but the sergeant ignored me and took his lunch break. Show me what to do. Amen." It had been so long since Hound Dog had prayed, and he didn't know what to do after you say amen and asked, "Is this where I cross myself? I didn't even close my eyes since I was driving. Does the prayer still count?"

A few minutes later Hound Dog was pulling into the parking space, and Johnny Handsome was getting some groceries out of his trunk.

"Hey, Hound Dog. Looks like you got a new ride!" said Johnny enthusiastically.

"Yeah, I'm borrowing it from a friend," said Hound Dog sheepishly.

And then it struck Hound Dog like a load of bricks, *I can talk to Johnny Handsome about what to do!*

Chapter 48- You Saw Hound Dog!

Detective Fortnight was irked to find out that Maurice "Hound Dog" Jackson's wanted poster was missing from the precinct's front bulletin board, so he printed off another copy. As the detective gathered the poster from the printer the sergeant that was on duty around lunch time took a second look at it.

"Hey, Fortnight!" yelled the sergeant, "Let me take a look at that poster."

Fortnight obliged the sergeant, and said, "Sure, knock yourself out."

The sergeant squinted and leaned his head to the side as he peered at the poster for about twenty seconds before starting to shake his head up and down, but not saying anything.

Fortnight couldn't take the suspense any longer, "Rick, what's going on? Spit it out!"

"This guy was in here today. He said he wanted to confess to beating up three cops on Friday morning," said the sergeant in a kicking himself fashion.

"What did you tell him?" asked Fortnight excitedly. He was desperate for anything, any clue that could help spring the case back open.

"I told him to lay off the sauce."

Chapter 49- A Real Godsend

Hound Dog realized Johnny Handsome was a former cop and a trusted neighbor; he had to talk to him about this new turn of events. But he also felt nervous about being outside and said, "Let me help you with those groceries and we can catch up at your place."

"Sure, Hound Dog, I'd love the help," replied Johnny Handsome.

Ten minutes later the two of them were sitting in Johnny Handsome's small apartment, and Hound Dog had a chance to relate the whole predicament to him: "Hang in there with me as I am trying to figure out this whole situation. And I'll start from the beginning."

Johnny Handsome was tracking and said, "Tell me every detail; I'm all ears."

"Okay, last Friday morning we started recording a new album in the Tri-City Records recording studio and were interrupted by three policemen that burst through some kind of hole in the wall. They were yelling and screaming at us to stop, and I lost my temper and beat all three of them up. After that I went on the run. I traded in my car and even got a fake driver's license and social security card and drove off to northern Indiana. The car I got was evidently owned by some crooked cop that stashed a ton of drugs in a secret trunk compartment. And evidently it was hot stuff because some criminals came to steal it. They were all caught and someone in Chicago sent them to get it."

Johnny asked a small question, "So what are you doing back here in Chicago?"

"Well, that's the funny part. I befriended a local sheriff on the account of his daughter being the most beautiful woman in the world," said Hound Dog.

The last part was heard by Johnny's wife Louise, so she blurted out, "No, I live in Chicago."

Johnny digressed as he responded, "That's right Sugarplum!" and then caught himself, "I'm sorry, Hound Dog; please continue."

"No problem. Well the sheriff said I needed to get these legal issues straightened out before I could pursue a relationship with his daughter, so I came back today to turn myself in for beating up the three cops last Friday. But here is the crazy part, when I tried to confess the crime the sergeant looked at me like I was some half-insane drunk. So I was starting to make my way out of the precinct and that's when I saw this," holding up the wanted poster for Johnny Handsome to see for himself.

Johnny Handsome read over it quickly and said, "This explains why the detectives were over to your place a couple of times. They were looking for evidence that you were this bank robber. I put their cards on my desk."

"I didn't rob a bank! But I know I beat up three policemen last Friday," complained Hound Dog.

Then Johnny asked an astute question, "What if those guys weren't policemen?"

"Then I let my temper get the best of me, and I was running away for nothing!" answered Hound Dog.

"No, you weren't running away for nothing. Someone wanted you to run, so you could look like the guilty culprit to the bank robbery," retorted Johnny.

"Man, I've been played like a fool!"

Chapter 50- Precinct Blues

The sergeant felt awful when he had both Detectives Fortnight and Cole breathing down his neck. And he couldn't believe that a wanted felon would just walk into the precinct and want to confess to committing a major crime. The only excuse he could offer was unsatisfactory, but he said it anyway, "I was hungry. I don't think straight when I get low blood sugar."

"It looks like you were only thinking about how to get your fill of Chunky's Burger Boy," answered Cole.

"I can't believe that he would come in here; this Hound Dog dude has guts," reasoned Fortnight.

"And he even took his own poster off the wall; the nerve of this guy," added Cole as he saw the "theft" of the poster as more of an insult than anything else.

Fortnight was starting to get really angry and said, "I can't wait to get my paws on this guy; I'll show him how to respect the law."

Chapter 51- He's Not Only Handsome, He's Smart Too

Johnny Handsome sat quietly for a few minutes mulling over all that Hound Dog had told him—trying to put all of the pieces together in his mind. Things weren't adding up, so he asked Hound Dog a question: "Let's talk about the criminals that were caught in Indiana; how in the world did they know your car was there?"

"The sheriff in Santiago figures that the crooks were leaning on my friend, Lightning Watkins to tell them of my whereabouts," answered Hound Dog as he took out the thick envelope that the sheriff had given to him. "The sheriff mentioned a Chicago phone number that kept calling one of the criminals; I think he wrote it down in this letter."

"Let me see it," asked Johnny.

Hound Dog opened up the envelope and discovered why it was so thick. Inside there was the letter to Hound Dog, Jupiter's phone details (IMSI and IMEI numbers), the Chicago phone number that had been calling and texting repeatedly, and an official document with a bag stapled to it.

"What's this all about?" asked Hound Dog.

Johnny examined it and aptly surmised, "This is some official evidence concerning the drugs that were in your car. It is all officially pronounced to grant you distance from it. This could be very helpful for you in the future."

Holding the paper with all the cell phone details, Johnny said, "I need to get in touch with a guy over at Chicago Telecom; he'll know what to do with these numbers. He's a pro by the name of M.C. Greene, but he goes by the name of "Wires" for short."

"Johnny, I'm really appreciative for all your help," said Hound Dog sincerely.

Chapter 52- Tiffany's Letter

While Johnny went to go talk on the phone with "Wires", Hound Dog took the opportunity to read the hand-written letter from Tiffany. The note still smelled like a fruity perfume and Hound Dog savored it because it brought back sweet memories of being with Tiffany and her dad as the constant chaperone.

Hound Dog opened up Tiffany's letter to read:

Dear Maurice,

It seems like a blur since I met you last Saturday morning at the diner. I'm already getting used to seeing you often even though we just met. I really hope that you will be able to return to Santiago soon, and that you won't have to go to jail.

Ever since our conversation on Sunday afternoon I've wanted to share with you some thoughts that have helped shape my view of life. Our conversation about God's undeserved mercy toward us is really important because salvation is a free gift. Some Christian groups want to put requirements in front of it, and other groups want to put requirements at the back end of it, but that doesn't make it a free gift anymore.

I can tell that a lot of these ideas are new to you, and may seem contrary to the way that the world operates. Many other religious worldviews are based on working one's way towards perfection, but I feel that is impossible. Still some people in the church hold on to this works mentality and it only produces pride and arrogance. On the other extreme are the people who know they have messed up and are constantly berating themselves. Both of these camps are not accepting God's perfect love.

132

Our friendship will not be changed whether you accept these truths or not, but I must tell you that I am saving myself for a man who will hold firmly to these same truths. In other words, I don't want you to make a decision to follow Jesus because of me; it has to be something you want to

Your friend,
Tiffany Baker

Hound Dog sat there reflecting on Tiffany's words and thought to himself, *What a woman; I'm glad she was upfront with me.* But before he could think more about the most beautiful woman in the world Johnny came back from his phone call with "Wires" Greene.

"Good news," said Johnny rubbing his hands together, "Wires is on top of things. He will get back with us if he has anything interesting to report on the numbers you provided. He is like a miniature National Security Agency for the Chicago metropolitan area; he hears everything once you log him onto the right path. Just you wait!" assured Johnny.

Hound Dog didn't know what to expect, but as long as it got the police off his tail he would be happy.

Chapter 53- House Call

Speaking of police, Detectives Fortnight and Cole decided to see if Hound Dog had come back home. They were across the hall knocking on Hound Dog's apartment door.

"Hound Dog, are you in there? Open up, it's the police," said Cole with authority.

Hound Dog and Johnny looked at each other with a look that communicated: *Maybe they will try this door next.*

Hound Dog gathered up his belongings, and he and Sasha quietly scampered to Johnny and Louise's bedroom to find a place to hide under their bed. It was full of old rugs and dusty boxes, but they were able to press themselves under the bed sufficiently. Fortunately, Louise was a fan of bed skirts, so it helped hide them. Hound Dog started thinking about how he always wanted to train Sasha to act like a stuffed wolf trophy. He would give the command "stuffed", and she could gnarl up her teeth and act like she was shot right before drawing blood. It would be a great party trick.

When the doorbell rang, Hound Dog recollected his thoughts and listened intently to the conversation from the living room.

Johnny answered the door enthusiastically, "Oh, hello Detectives. Don't tell me, don't tell me..." scratching his head, "Detectives Portfight and Bowl! Is that right?"

"Close, it's Fortnight and Cole," answered Fortnight.

"Now, which is which, are you Fortbight and you're Pole?" asked Johnny.

This was starting to frustrate the detectives, because a name is special to a person. And Fortnight answered first, "I'm Detective Fortnight, and we were wondering if you've seen Maurice Jackson around."

Johnny did his best stalling, "Let me think…" complete with head scratching.

The detectives didn't have any patience so they moved on to another question to help make it easier for Johnny to answer. Cole asked, "Have you seen Hound Dog inside his apartment?"

It was just around this time that Hound Dog was having a strong urge to sneeze, and he was trying every trick in the book to not let it happen. Hound Dog's mind started raced with random thoughts: *What would happen if Sasha released gas under the bed? I would be asphyxiated. Then the detectives would eventually find me dead under Johnny and Louise's bed, and the courts would send them to prison for the rest of their lives.*

Hound Dog's attention returned to the front door conversation, Johnny had intentionally confused the detectives' questions and was making quite a nuisance of himself, "Well of course, I've seen Hound Dog in his apartment, we've been neighbors for eight years. Now what is so confusing about that?"

The detectives were getting nowhere with this senile old man, so they decided they better leave and keep looking elsewhere. Cole concluded the conversation by saying, "Thanks for your time Mr. Handsome. Here are our cards if you ever need to reach us."

Taking the cards in his hands Johnny said, "Oh, thank you, detectives."

Chapter 54- Love Advice

After the excitement of the unexpected visitors Hound Dog and Sasha came out from underneath the bed and rejoined Johnny and Louise in the living room. Hound Dog was feeling a little sore from being crammed under the bed, but Sasha was as right as rain because wolves can enjoy tight, crammed spaces that would induce claustrophobia in most humans.

Louise greeted Hound Dog by saying, "We've been just awful hosts; would you like some coffee or tea?"

"Just some coffee would be great, thank you," answered Hound Dog.

"How about you honey: coffee, tea, or *me*?" asked Louise.

"Oh, I'll take you anytime, baby," answered Johnny, coming over to kiss her hand and arm, and saying, *"L'amour de ma vie!"* It was just like a scene out of the "Addam's Family".

"You guys really do love each other," remarked Hound Dog.

"Yes, we do," said Johnny, "We've been married almost fifty-six years. And it just keeps getting better. That's not to say it has always been sunshine and happy times; we've had our fair share of rough times and heartaches."

Hound Dog asked Johnny, "How did you know Louise was *the* one?"

"Well, a real wise man asked me two questions when I was thinking about marrying Louise: The first question was, 'Do you think she is the most beautiful woman in the world?' and I said, 'Yes.' Then the second question was, 'Can you live without her?' and I said, 'No.' And after that it was pretty much settled."

"What do you mean by 'settled'?" asked Hound Dog.

Johnny thought for a moment, "I think the words of another wise man will answer your question when he said, 'Love is more a decision of the will than an emotion.'"

"That doesn't sound very romantic," complained Hound Dog.

"That's right, because loving someone takes daily commitment, and emotions come and go," answered Johnny.

Hound Dog sat there trying to connect his emotions towards Tiffany and the thoughts of lifelong commitment.

Johnny entered the uncomfortable silence and said, "Let me put it to you another way. A man doesn't wake up one morning and say to himself: 'I think I am going to have an affair today.' What happens is that the man makes small decisions that erode his commitment to his wife."

"That's wild, I haven't thought about it that way before," said Hound Dog as he contemplated their discussion.

"I'm going to run to the store; I will leave you here for a while to think things over and relax," said Johnny.

"Thanks, I could use a rest," answered Hound Dog.

Chapter 55- Wires Connected

The next day Johnny met "Wires" at the local pizza shop, Antonio's Flying Pizza House & Pawnshop. It is one of the rare places in the world where you can hock your grandmother's family heirlooms for a pizza or a calzone. After ordering a pizza, Johnny and Wires sat down together in the farthest booth they could find away from the other customers. Wires was used to working in the bowels of Chicago Telecom and didn't have a lot of interaction with people. The good news was that Johnny and Wires were old and trusted friends.

"Good to see you, Wires," said Johnny.

"I'm happy to see you, but I don't think you're going to like these results," said Wires shaking his head back and forth, "Your friend is in the midst of some serious criminal enterprise."

Johnny knew Wires was a straight-shooter, so he asked him, "What kind of trouble?"

"This is stuff for the narcotics boys, and big figures of cash being floated out there," said Wires looking around to make sure no one else was listening in to their conversation.

"Okay, I know this is serious; show me what you got," reassured Johnny.

Wires took out some print-outs from his closely guarded satchel and started explaining and sketching out a diagram, "The IMSI and IMEI numbers you gave me belong to a known criminal operative that goes by the moniker of Jupiter Links; he has a rap sheet longer than both of our arms put together. This is bad dude number one."

"Okay, I'm tracking," said Johnny.

138

"Looks like the Chicago number that has been trying desperately to get in touch with him, is some other criminal that sent Jupiter to do a job; that's bad dude number two. And this is where it gets even more complicated," said Wires pausing to take a breath.

"A bad dude number three is calling from two separate land lines in South Chicago, and he is disappointed that bad dude number one, Jupiter, is incommunicado. He is calling bad dude number two day and night for updates," said Wires as he illustrated the connection points on the paper.

"Okay, I see this. Tell me more," suggested Johnny.

"Now it gets really interesting because two very short calls have come to bad dude number three since you got me on this case. Both very brief calls, a little cryptic in nature, but very much indicative of a heavy debt to be paid by bad dude number three." said Wires.

"Any idea where these calls are coming from?" asked Johnny.

Wires proceeded to talk in a low whisper, "That's the scary part— there coming from Westmoor Heights—from Canton's estate to be exact."

"What about bad dude number three? Those were landlines, right?" asked Johnny.

"One is from some defunct record label called Tri-City Records, and the other must be his residence near Pinworthy and West 49th Street. Tri-City must be some type of front operation," said Wires confidently.

"No way, this is going to break Hound Dog's heart," said Johnny.

"Here, take these print-outs. All the details are there, including the transcribed phone calls and text messages. It's all there," said Wires.

"Thanks, Wires for all your help; I better get back to Hound Dog with these results," said Johnny as he gathered up the data and got up to leave.

"What about the pizza?" asked Wires.

"Knock yourself out! You earned it. I gotta' go."

Chapter 56- The Truth Hurts

When Johnny got back to his apartment Hound Dog, Louise and Sasha were all in the living room watching TV. Hound Dog tends to watch TV when he is stressed-out, especially reruns of cheesy sitcoms. Johnny decided to let them finish the episode of "Hogan's Heroes" before he broke the news to Hound Dog.

Hound Dog was too nervous to ask about the meeting with Wires, but in the back of his mind he knew it wasn't going to be pretty. He thought to himself, *I bet Johnny is going to tell me something like, 'Hound Dog, you are stuck in the middle of a giant DEA sting operation called OPERATION RACCOON SKIN. You have 24 hours to make it to Canada before the authorities come to take you away and throw you into Terre Haute Federal Prison for the rest of your life.'*

Johnny approached Hound Dog and said, "I got some bad news for you."

"Tell it to me straight, don't sugar coat it," replied Hound Dog.

"I'm not going to beat around the bush; don't worry about that. I'll tell you like it is and not dance around trying to ignore the giant elephant under the rug," said Johnny.

Hound Dog was getting impatient, "Will you just spit it out!"

"Someone at Tri-City Records framed you for the bank heist," said Johnny.

"What? That's impossible!" exclaimed Hound Dog.

"It gets worse. Looks like they were involved in some heavy drug trafficking as well, and they're actually tied to the drugs you found in the back of the former cop car," said Johnny.

141

"What? Tri-City Records isn't running drugs; they make music," said Hound Dog resisting Johnny's accusation.

Johnny took out the print-outs from Wires and started reading them over as Hound Dog sat there ruminating over this bad news for what seemed minutes on end.

Finally, after about ten minutes of silence Johnny spoke up and said, "I think I have a way to get you out of this predicament."

Chapter 57- Anonymous Anonymous

Johnny broke out an old, raggedy pre-paid cell phone and blew the dust off the battery before placing it into the phone. In his other hand he fingered Detective Cole's card as the phone booted up.

Johnny asked Hound Dog, "You haven't had any conversations with the detectives, right?"

"No, I haven't talked to them at all. And I don't want to; they're out to get me," answered Hound Dog.

"Well, they know my voice from previous conversations, so I can't do it," said Johnny.

"Here, give it to me; I'll call them and tell them your message!" said Louise.

Johnny pointed to something he had written down previously as Louise dialed the phone number.

The number rang, and Detective Cole answered, "This is Detective Cole."

Then in the most perfect and freaky hostage-taker voice she muffled out, "Meet me at the midnight opening of 'Martian Invasion IV' at the Drake Theatre on Henry and West 5th Street," before quickly clicking off the phone call and powering it off.

"Wow, honey, I didn't know you could do that creepy voice," said Johnny.

"I raised three children; I can do anything!" answered Louise.

Chapter 58- Does this Satureenan Mechzoid Suit Make Me Look Fat?

The next thing Hound Dog knew he was at Crazy Sal's Costume Universe on West 45th and River Lane. Johnny was excited about the prospect of picking out the most radical alien costume he could find.

Hound Dog wasn't too excited about wearing a costume; he was a Blues magician and had his standards, "I'll look so silly dressed up like some freak."

"C'mon Hound Dog, how many times in your life do you get to dress up like some extra-terrestrial creature from the planet Zorkon?" said Johnny chiding, "Besides, no one will know it's you."

"Okay, okay, I'll put something on," responded Hound Dog, and then in a fatalistic tone, "I'm sure we won't have any costume parties in prison."

Johnny didn't like that defeatist tone and told Hound Dog, "You are NOT going to prison; we're going to get you off the meat hook. You hear me?"

"I hear you; and I hope this works," said Hound Dog.

Chapter 59- Night of the Living Martians

"Here we are, opening night of the 'Night of the Living Martians' at the Drake," said Detective Cole.

"We're a little early; I hope this anonymous caller shows up," replied Detective Fortnight, "Anyway, let's go buy our tickets."

The detectives made their way to the ticket booth to purchase their tickets, and Cole remarked, "Will you get a load of this; everybody and their dog are decked out as Martian characters and extra-terrestrials."

"Yeah, everybody but us!" responded Fortnight as he was feeling out of place.

"This is just great! How are we supposed to recognize anyone when they are all dressed up like aliens!" remarked Cole.

$$* \qquad * \qquad * \qquad * \qquad * \qquad * \qquad * \qquad *$$

The Drake movie theatre usually keeps people crowded in the foyer area before the start of a big show. It helps build the excitement and helps popcorn sales. Johnny had calculated this delay perfectly on the night of a big premier of a science-fiction thriller.

From Johnny and Hound Dog's vantage point they could see the detectives looking lost and agitated in the milieu of strange and outlandish life forms.

Johnny leaned over to Hound Dog and said, "Let's wait a few more minutes for the lobby to get really packed before we deliver our message."

"I'll follow your lead," responded Hound Dog.

$$* \qquad * \qquad * \qquad * \qquad * \qquad * \qquad * \qquad *$$

Indeed, the detectives were feeling uncomfortable as people would jostle by them and poke them with horns or light sabers.

"I don't like the look of this situation," remarked Fortnight.

"Hang in there, this could really pan out for us," said Cole more optimistically.

*   *   *   *   *   *   *   *

Johnny recognized the point where the foyer was packed like a Hong Kong subway on Chinese New Year and the ushers were just about to let everybody into the theatre. He tapped Hound Dog and said, "Let's do it."

Hound Dog followed Johnny as he bobbed his large Zorkon warrior suit towards the detectives. Hound Dog readied a large envelope with double-sided tape on it. He was wearing large costume gloves to mask any fingerprints. Fortunately the detectives were facing the direction of the ushers. It was crowded and tight and the detectives were getting pushed towards the theatre entryway; they tried to stand their ground, resisting the flow of traffic.

Johnny forced his way in front of the detectives knowing that they would be distracted by the iridescent wings and copious amounts of glitter. This was Hound Dog's chance to stick the envelope onto the larger detective and slip back into the crowd unnoticed.

Cole and Fortnight were soon the only ones standing in the empty foyer with the ushers wondering why the two patrons had not gone in to the theatre.

Cole spoke up first, "Looks like this whole adventure was a bust; let's get out of here."

And as Cole turned towards the door, Fortnight noticed the large envelope stuck to Cole's back.

"Hold on there; you have something on your back," said Fortnight as he reached to tear it off of the back of Cole's coat.

Fortnight feverishly opened it up and found a typed out note and a bag of white powder. The note read:

Detectives,

Thanks for taking the risk in showing up tonight!

In roughly 27 hours from now a group from Canton's criminal outfit will meet another group of criminals that are going to make payment for a large drug shipment that was interdicted by a crooked cop. You will find the drug sample in this envelope matches a shipment recently turned over to the authorities in Santiago, Indiana.

The payment is scheduled for 3 am, early Thursday morning at the vacant lot on West 39th and Grand Avenue. I venture to guess that you will be able to recover $2.6 million of the $4 million stolen from the 3rd National Bank of Chicago.

Be safe out there,

Hound Dog

The detectives couldn't believe their eyes; if this letter from Hound Dog was true they were virtually having the case dropped into their laps.

"Man, the chief is going to be elated when he sees this," said Detective Fortnight.

"I can see it now. Front page headline: 'Chicago's Finest Make Bust of the Year!'" exclaimed Cole.

Chapter 60- The Doubting Chief

The next morning Chief Dixon wasn't thrilled about what the detectives showed him, and he let the detectives know it: "You two jokers mean to tell me the guy you pinned down as the lead suspect, this Hound Dog character, is now your main source. What are you guys thinking? For that matter: Are you even thinking?"

Detective Cole explained, "Chief, we've had to back pedal on this guy because there's more to this story than we thought. We revisited with Sergeant Miller about what happened when Hound Dog came into the precinct on Monday around lunch time."

But the chief interrupted and spoke in his usual heated manner, "What? Are you telling me this key suspect was in my precinct and we didn't grab him! Does anybody tell me what is going on around here?"

Cole continued, "Hold on a minute. Sergeant Miller said that Hound Dog came and confessed to beating up three cops on Friday morning. And the sergeant knew for certain that three of our men were not assaulted on Friday morning, so he thought Hound Dog was drunk and sent him on his way."

The chief's eyes narrowed and he started thinking for a moment, "Do you mean some crooks were impersonating Chicago Police officers and have framed Hound Dog?"

Cole answered with a resolute "Yes, sir."

But the chief wasn't buying it, "And how in the world does he know specific details about a big payoff happening tonight?"

Detective Fortnight, "That's a great question, and we still haven't figured out how he knows these details."

But this only made the chief even angrier, "Don't patronize me; I know it is a good question since I asked it. And while you're working on that question, think about this one: what charges are you going to bring on all of these criminals for when you catch them? Passing large sums of money in a public place?"

Cole spoke up, "We've been cooperating with the narcotics guys to see what Canton and his operation have been up to. Hopefully, they have some information from wire taps or the Kartow investigation."

The chief had heard enough from his detectives, and he dismissed them by saying, "Man, now I have heard it all! Now get out of here!"

Chapter 61- A Matter of Faith

Hound Dog had now spent a couple of nights with the Handsome family and had lots of time to observe Johnny and Louise's lives. Louise was nice enough to take Sasha out on periodic walks during the day, and Johnny would take Sasha out at night.

Hound Dog shared meals with the couple and found out more about them that he hadn't known as their neighbor for eight years. Johnny had come to see a show or two of Hound Dog's, but he really didn't know him deeply. For starters he had learned how much they loved each other still after so many years of marriage, and now he was learning about their faith since Johnny and Louise regularly prayed before their meals.

"All these years living next door to you, and I didn't know you guys were Christians," remarked Hound Dog as they shared lunch together in their small dining area inside the kitchen.

"Are you a Christian, Hound Dog?" asked Louise.

"I don't know; I am just trying to figure out things for myself right now," answered Hound Dog, "My mom took me to church when I was a kid, but I didn't like what I saw in the church—lots of hypocrisy."

Louise spoke up, "I think you're right; but there are hypocrites in every facet of society, including the church, since none of us live out our values perfectly."

"How about you Johnny, how do you know your faith is real?" asked Hound Dog.

Johnny sat back and thought for a moment before saying, "You know as a cop I saw the lowest and cruelest acts of men and women, and that convinced me of the existence of evil. On the flipside, I also saw the most humane and caring acts of men and women, and those acts convince me of the existence of real love. And those two ideas match up with what the Bible says about the hearts of people around the world."

Hound Dog challenged him again with another question, "But how could God create a world with so much suffering and pain; doesn't God love us?"

Johnny answered him, "Yes, God really does love us. He entered into this world of suffering and pain and lived among us."

"You know you're the second person who has said that to me recently, and I just don't see how it all fits together right now," responded Hound Dog.

"Maybe you can think about it reading the teachings of Jesus Christ for yourself," suggested Johnny.

Chapter 62- Afternoon Situation Report

At four in the afternoon Chief Dixon called Detective Cole's cell to see if he had answered the questions from the morning. The good news was that the boss was in a cheerful mood this time.

"Tell it to me straight detective; what you got?" said the chief as if they were playing poker together.

Cole picked up this good vibe and told the chief: "Do you want the good news or the best news, first?"

"Go ahead, hit me with your best shot," answered the chief.

"Today we got in touch with the sheriff in Santiago, and he thinks Hound Dog is legitimate. He gave us details on how Hound Dog turned in the drugs and came back to Chicago to turn himself in for assaulting three policemen. That's the whole reason he ran away," explained the detective.

"Okay, that sounds good; what's the other news?" asked the chief.

"We talked with the owner of the vacant lot, and he is willing to press charges for criminal trespassing when we catch Canton's men and this other crew on the premises," said Cole.

"I like the sound of that, and that will give us a chance to trace the money to see if it is really from the 3rd National Bank of Chicago," agreed the chief.

"We still have no idea how Hound Dog found out about this meeting, but we feel confident that we can arrest these guys tonight, separate them for interrogation, and put some criminals in jail for the night," said Cole optimistically.

"That should make for a long night. Do you have the arrest plan laid out for the vacant lot?" asked the chief.

"Yes, we do. We were planning on getting some rest early and then take our assigned positions before we execute the arrest." answered Cole.

"That sounds like a plan. You guys be careful tonight. I don't want to see any body bags with you in them," said the chief in a more morbid tone.

"Alright chief, we will give you a report in the morning," said the detective.

"Good, see you in the morning." signed off the chief.

Cole talking to Fortnight said, "I think the chief has some type of multiple personality disorder. He was a grouch this morning, but on the phone just now he was bright and actually pleasant. You'd think he just won the lottery by the way he was talking to me."

"I think he's crazy, but I'm not a trained psychologist," replied Fortnight.

Chapter 63- A Visit to Slick

When Slick was closing up his business for the night he had welcome visitors: Johnny and Hound Dog.

"Hey guys; good to see you both," said Slick.

"Good to see you," answered Johnny.

"Hey, Hound Dog, did you ever get my message about the money I found in your car?" asked Slick.

"No, but I could always use some," replied Hound Dog.

"I got it right here in my little cubby-hole. Even those lousy detectives couldn't find this spot," said Slick, taking out the $10,000 bundle in its distinctive 3rd National Bank of Chicago wrapping.

"What detectives are you talking about?" asked Johnny, "are their names Fortnight and Cole."

"No, not those guys, they were great. It was the second couple of detectives that came and roughed me up and took all my paperwork; they were a couple of real jerks," answered Slick.

Johnny then spoke to Hound Dog, "Sounds like the same group of guys that you met in the Tri-City Records recording studio—thugs that impersonate policemen."

"That's the funny thing, after I called Lightning Watkins at Tri-City those fake detectives showed up at my place," said Slick.

"You know after I phoned Lightning Watkins a group of auto thieves came to steal the cop car you sold me," added Hound Dog.

"Looks like we need to make a visit to see Lightning Watkins tonight," said Johnny as he was thinking about something, "And Slick, if you wouldn't mind joining us, we might need that big Ford truck over there and three or four tow chains."

Slick answered enthusiastically, "Sure, the beast is always available—any way to get back at those creeps."

Chapter 64- You're Busted

The detectives and a small contingent of plain clothes policemen had taken their assigned positions in concealment around the vacant lot at West 39th and Grand Avenue. Detectives Fortnight and Cole were situated in a panel van serving as the command post. They had patrol cars at the ready to bring in a uniformed presence and even a police helicopter in the area for overhead surveillance. Everyone was on radio silence and awaiting the "ready" and "go" signs from Cole.

Fortnight and Cole were talking casually until they noticed a black Cadillac Escalade roll casually into the vacant lot two minutes before 3 am. The Cadillac driver situated the rear of the vehicle so as to readily transfer the pay-off.

Fortnight was first to notice it and said, "Looks like we got one party on the lot."

"It takes two to tango, and I sure hope the other crew shows up," answered Cole.

One minute later a black Dodge Charger drove by the lot and turned on to Grand Avenue, but was back in another thirty seconds.

Cole recognized that it was the same car that drove by at 2 am, "Looks like this guy has been pulling surveillance detection runs; these guys are good."

Fortnight was speaking out loud to provide commentary for the video camera, "The Dodge Charger is pulling into the vacant lot, and turning for the trunk to face the rear of the Cadillac."

     *   *   *   *   *   *   *   *

Clayton was feeling nervous and a little jittery about handing off this massive amount of cash to Canton's men. His previous drives around the neighborhood hadn't revealed any hidden traps or people around, just a couple of homeless people. Clayton reminded himself, *I've got nothing to worry about—we are just delivering cash to pay a debt.*

Trigger and Sparky were in the back seat. They were tired and ready to go to bed.

Trigger spoke up, "Clayton, are you ready for us to go, yet?"

"I'm going to pop the trunk, you each take a duffle bag over to the Escalade," answered Clayton, "And remember, no sudden movements that will spook them."

With those instructions, Clayton popped the trunk release and Sparky and Trigger each got out of the car from their respective sides.

＊　　＊　　＊　　＊　　＊　　＊　　＊　　＊

Upon seeing the back car doors open, Cole gave the "Ready" sign to get the arrest team alert. The helicopter in the area moved to within visual distance to keep an eye on things from above if the arrest got hairy.

Fortnight kept talking the event through as the video camera recorded the events for the prosecutors to have in the future, "Two suspects are carrying the bags they got out of the Charger's trunk and are approaching the rear of the Cadillac Escalade. Two people have come out of the Cadillac Escalade and are opening the back door."

This was the moment when Cole gave the "Go!" signal and the cops came out of the woodwork and entered into the video frame.

＊　　＊　　＊　　＊　　＊　　＊　　＊　　＊

When Clayton heard the abrupt orders of the police to freeze his fight or flight instincts to run went into overdrive. He put the Charger in gear and slammed down the accelerator pedal with all of his strength. He was careful to avoid hitting the police so they wouldn't shoot at him in self-defense. As he peered back through the rear-view mirror he saw that Canton's men, along with Trigger and Sparky were already on the ground with cops swarming all over them.

Clayton had chosen this vacant lot over others available because of the multiple exits available to him. The last thing he wanted to be was a cornered rat.

*   *   *   *   *   *   *   *

"Looks like we have a runner!" reported Cole into the radio, "Chopper 9-Chopper 9, come in, over"

"This is Chopper 9, I have the suspect in sight; suspect is heading north on Grand, over," reported the police helicopter.

"I bet he is heading towards the interstate," said Cole to Fortnight, and then on the radio, "Calling cars 2-Niner, 5-Niner, and 9-Niner. Be on the lookout for a Black Dodge Charger heading your way, over."

"This is 2-Niner, I have a visual and I am in hot pursuit. Suspect is moving, pushing 100 miles per hour, over," responded 2-Niner on the radio.

"This is 9-Niner, I am joining the pursuit, over," responded 9-Niner.

*   *   *   *   *   *   *   *

Clayton was pushing the envelope and was racing as fast as he could to get to the interstate. He turned off the air conditioning to see if that would give him a little boost of horsepower. Clayton's adrenaline was pumping and his heart was racing as he ran through red light after red light. He had to put as much distance between himself and the cops.

Before he realized it, he had two cop cars behind him, and it looked like a third car was going to try and pull out in front of him. Clayton touched the brakes lightly, turned the wheel hard, and punched the accelerator. It looked like he was heading the wrong way down a one way street, so he cut down an alleyway to see if he could get back on Grand Avenue and on to one of the highways.

The Charger's engine was redlining and Clayton knew he wasn't out of the woods, yet. Then he realized that one of the police cars had followed him down the alleyway. Before he knew it he was approaching the end of the alleyway as it came to a new street. Clayton raced the car out of the alleyway and right into the path of a delivery truck. There was no time to react.

"No!" screamed Clayton as the truck hit him square on and discharged the Charger's airbags. The car had so much forward momentum that it spun and careened into light pole.

The first police car to the report was 2-Niner, "This is 2-Niner. The suspect has crashed. I repeat, the suspect has crashed. Request an ambulance to a location 100 yards east of the West 12th Street and Grand Avenue intersection, over."

The policemen came to the scene of the car crash and found Clayton unconscious. The delivery driver still couldn't believe that the car had raced out in front of him, and the police reassured him that it wasn't his fault.

*   *   *   *   *   *   *   *

Back at the vacant lot Fortnight and Cole were congratulating themselves on a successful arrest. All of the cash in the duffel bags had tight bindings from the 3rd National Bank of Chicago. The suspects were taken back to the 9th Precinct in separate cars so that they couldn't collaborate on false alibis.

"Looks like we got some guys that will have some explaining to do in the interrogation rooms tonight," said Fortnight.

Cole agreed, "Tell the precinct to fire up the coffee pot; it's going to be a long night."

Chapter 65- Sweet Redemption

It was thirty minutes past the scheduled payoff time, and a lone figure on the third floor at Tri-City Records was getting very nervous. Lightning Watkins was thinking to himself, *Why haven't they called, yet? What could have gone wrong? Maybe Clayton and his goons skipped town with the cash.*

In the midst of his delirium the phone rang.

Lightning spoke his relief aloud, "Finally, some confirmation," as he picked up the phone before the first ring could even finish, and said, "I've been waiting for almost half an hour to hear from you. Why didn't you call earlier?"

Lightning didn't expect to hear Hound Dog's voice on the other end say to him, "Were you expecting someone calling to tell you that your payoff to Canton went through without a hitch?"

And without thinking Lightning said, "Yes. Um... I mean no way."

"You dirty rat; you were going to send me to prison to cover for your bank heist!" exclaimed Hound Dog.

"Now Hound Dog, don't let your temper get the worst of you. I was using the money to help keep Tri-City afloat," explained Lightning, "If we don't use the money Tri-City Records will go under; you know Al was barely making payroll until I got us some help from Canton."

"You didn't help anybody, but yourself!" shouted Hound Dog angrily.

That was when Lightning realized that he was hearing Hound Dog's voice from the phone receiver and from somewhere below him, so he asked, "Where are you, Hound Dog?"

162

"I'm inside Tri-City Records, and I'm coming to get you. I'm going to put a stop to this criminal enterprise tonight," said Hound Dog emphatically.

Lightning took this as a challenge and yelled back, "Oh, yeah! You and what army?"

There was no answer from Hound Dog on the other end, so Lightning slammed down the phone and started listening for sounds of movement.

Hound Dog yelled from the second floor, "It's all over Lightning; it's time to give yourself up."

Lightning fumbled through the back of his desk drawer to find a large .38 revolver and a box of shells, and yelled out at Hound Dog, "Come and get me, Hound Dog!" As he nervously loaded the revolver he could hear Hound Dog coming up the steps and some other odd noise. He quickly thought to himself, *it's probably that lousy mutt of his coming up the stairs as well. It will be nice to put it out of its misery. Plus, one less Blues singer.*

Hound Dog came to the top of the stairs with a handful of vinyl records in his left hand and one ready to throw in his right hand. Sasha was crouched low behind Hound Dog on the steps. When Hound Dog saw Lightning at his desk he let the record fly at him.

The flying record caught Lightning off guard, and he squeezed off a round in the direction of Hound Dog. Fortunately, Hound Dog had two things working in his favor: Number one, Hound Dog had already ducked back into the stairwell; number two, Lightning was an awful shot.

Outside of the Tri-City Records building Johnny and Slick heard the report of the gunshot. They decided to go and see if they could help Hound Dog. One of the drawbacks of vigilante justice was that they couldn't phone the police.

Hound Dog knew he and Sasha could take Lightning once he was disarmed, so he threw another vinyl record at him to see if he could get him to expend his ammunition. This record actually hit Lightning, and in response Lightning fired off two more shots in Hound Dog's general direction. One shot was actually pretty close to hitting him, and Hound Dog feared the ricochet off the brick walls.

Hound Dog made a three symbol to reaffirm in his mind that Lightning had three shots left and then threw two successive records at Lightning who at this point was up on his feet and getting closer to the stairwell.

Both records hit Lightning and only angered him more than ever, and he yelled, "I'm going to kill you Hound Dog!" as he made his way towards the stairwell.

Hound Dog knew it was time to go for broke because Lightning's chances of hitting him were a lot better at short distance, so he chunked the remaining stack of records at Lightning and bomb-rushed him. One of the records hit Lightning in the face and another hit his hand and skewed the aim of his pistol. He let off a shot, but he was nowhere close to hitting Hound Dog.

Hound Dog came up underneath Lightning and tackled him and pushed Lightning's right wrist and forearm away from himself.

Lightning tried in vain to shoot at Hound Dog two more times. He was now out of bullets.

Sasha then reacted to the danger to her master and came in to attack Lightning as well. Lightning's life would have been history if Hound Dog had not ordered Sasha calmly, "Just hold him down Sasha." And with that order, Sasha kept her teeth securely on Lightning's neck.

At this time, Slick and Johnny arrived to find out that Hound Dog had survived the gunshots. They were relieved to say the least and said, "Thank goodness you are alright, Hound Dog."

Hound Dog didn't even respond to Johnny and Slick since he was focused on getting the truth out of Lightning and spoke to Lightning firmly: "One sudden move and Sasha will break your neck like a twig. Now answer this question: where is the rest of the bank's money that wasn't used for tonight's payoff?"

Lightning was squeamish with the jaws of death perched on his jugular, so he answered timidly, "The rest of the money is in the records collection on the second floor."

Hound Dog continued to give the orders, "I am going to remove Sasha from your neck and you are going to take me to the rest of the money and we are going to take it to your car outside. Do you understand me?"

Lightning gave a sheepish reply, "Y-yes, Hound Dog."

Hound Dog gave Sasha the command, "Sasha, release."

The defeated Lightning led the way downstairs to the records collection and showed Hound Dog two duffel bags packed tightly with cash.

Hound Dog didn't want to have any of his fingerprints anywhere close to the bags, so he ordered Lightning to pick both of them up and take them outside. Lightning strained under the weight, but did admirably carrying the load out to his 7-series BMW. It must have been the adrenaline.

Hound Dog was still giving the orders and told Lightning, "Open your trunk, put the duffel bags in there, and give me the keys."

Lightning obeyed begrudgingly.

"Now climb into the trunk also," ordered Hound Dog as he threw in the $10,000 into the trunk that Slick had found in the Mark III.

"But I will suffocate in there," complained Lightning.

"That's okay, you can tell the police all about it," scoffed Hound Dog.

Lightning reluctantly climbed into the trunk and laid in between an estimated $1.4 million in hard cash.

Chapter 66- Late Night Delivery

Four minutes later Hound Dog, Sasha, and Johnny all were riding in Slick's giant Ford diesel dually dragging Lightning's BMW in tow. Slick kept the parking brake on so that it would offer some resistance and not allow the car to slide under his bumper if he had to stop. The parking brake sounded like a squealing banshee and they could only imagine what it sounded like in the trunk. The good news was that the streets were empty at 4 am and most people would be able to sleep through the awful racket.

"Turn up here on the right and we'll be able to dump Lightning's car in the precincts' employee parking lot," suggested Johnny to Slick.

"I wonder if there is going to be any rubber left on those tires after being pulled over the asphalt?" asked Slick.

"Where he's going I don't think he'll be too worried about tire life," responded Johnny.

Slick pulled into the employee's parking lot and slowed down so as to not make too much of a commotion and positioned the car in the most obvious spot—the precinct chief's reserved parking place.

Hound Dog jumped out of the crew cab door and helped Slick in removing the tow chains, but kept one tow chain wrapped around the trunk so Lightning couldn't escape by pulling the emergency trunk release. Hound Dog took out Lightning's car keys and stuck them in the trunk lock, and hopped back up into the crew cab.

Slick put the black beast into gear and rolled out of the lot, leaving the BMW behind.

Johnny holding up his trusty cell phone asked Hound Dog, "Would you like to do the honors? I'm sure the detectives would enjoy talking to you."

"No, why don't you make the call; this was your entire plan in the first place," replied Hound Dog.

"Okay, okay, I'll do it," said Johnny as he started dialing and waited for the line to connect, "Hello, Detective Porkplight!"

"This is Detective *Fortnight*," said with emphasis on the correct pronunciation.

"Hey, this is Johnny. I just left Toll and you a big present in the parking lot behind the precinct. Look for a sharp looking beamer in the chief's spot. The keys are already in the trunk for you to open it up."

Not really knowing what to say, and tired from a full night of police work Fortnight gave a lackadaisical response, "Okay... I'll go out to see what you left for me Johnny."

Johnny signed off in his chipper way by saying, "Sounds good Detective Nortfight; you go and get some sleep you sound exhausted, over and out."

Fortnight responded with, "Over and out, Johnny," he was too tired to care about correcting his name anymore. And he then called over to Detective Cole, "Hey Cole, we got some type of surprise in the back parking lot from Johnny Handsome. Something about a BMW parked in the chief's spot."

The two detectives proceeded to the back parking lot and found a BMW 7-series awkwardly filling the chief's parking space. Both of them went around to the trunk, unloosened the tow chain, and Fortnight unlocked the trunk. To their surprise they found Jeff "Lightning"

Watkins in the fetal position between two large duffel bags that looked distinctly like the duffel bags they recovered from tonight's arrests.

"He looks familiar; didn't he work at Tri-City Records?" asked Fortnight.

"I can explain everything," offered Lightning.

"I'm sure you can," said Fortnight in a reassuring manner.

"Let's take him in and see if any of our suspects recognize him as 'the boss' they have been crowing about since they got here," suggested Cole.

"Sounds good to me," answered Fortnight as they both bent over to grab Lightning out of the trunk space.

Chapter 67- Sweet Home Santiago

After a good, long sleep back in his own bed Hound Dog felt like a new man. He and Sasha were already on the interstate in Tiffany's Prius driving back to Santiago. If they hurried they might be able to make it in time for a late lunch at the diner.

Hound Dog had a lot to share about the last 48 hours of suspense and excitement to clear his name. He couldn't wait to tell her, but he still didn't want to get a speeding ticket. So to help him calm his nerves he turned on the radio and caught the tail end of one of his favorite songs: "Coming Home" by the Leroy Kasem. Hound Dog thought to himself, *How fitting*.

> *I'm coming home to you, baby,*
> *And I sure hope you'll take me in.*
> *Cause I been gone so long it's a shame,*
> *And I sure need your loving, baby.*
>
> *I never wanted to leave you, baby,*
> *And it hurt so much to be away.*
> *'Cause no one loves me the same,*
> *And I am so glad I am coming home to you, baby*

THE END

Appendix A

APPLICATION TO DATE MY BELOVED DAUGHTER

Name: _____
       (Last)   (First)   (Middle)

Aliases: _____

Date of Birth: _____
               (Day/Month/Year)

Birthplace: _____
          (City/County/State/Country)

EDUCATION & EAGLE SCOUT RESPONSE SECTION:
Circle or write in your responses.

1. Do you have a college degree from an accredited institution?

        YES   NO

2. Which university?

_____

3. Did you major in engineering or a physical science?

        YES   NO

4. Did you graduate _____ Cum Laude?

        Magna   Suma

5. Were you a member of a fraternity in university?

        YES   NO

6. Have you completed a master's degree?

        YES   NO

7. Are you an Eagle Scout?

        YES   NO

8. If NO, why not?

_____

9. If YES, what was your leadership project?

_____

DEFINITION SECTION: In as few words as possible define the terms below.

10. God

_____

11. Integrity

_____

12. Work

_____

13. Sacrifice

_____

14. Honor

_____

15. Chastity

_____

16. Guardian

_____

17. Death

_____

DISQUALIFICATION SECTION: Circle YES or NO.

18. Were any of the words in the DEFINITION SECTION unfamiliar

to you?   YES   NO

19. Have you ever been convicted of a felony offense?

YES   NO

20. If NO, have you ever been indicted for a felony offense?

YES   NO

21. At present, do you have any communicable diseases?

YES   NO

22. At present, are your immunizations up-to-date?

YES   NO

23. Have you registered for selective service?

YES   NO

24. Have you ever lied to you mother or father?

YES   NO

25. Have you lied about any of the above questions?

YES   NO

26. Which ones? _____

PURITY & RESPECT SHORT ANSWER SECTION:

Use the space provided to answer.

27. Is the curfew of 10pm (2200) ever to be broken? ___

28. Is our beloved daughter, _____, to be respected always? _____

29. Are you to ever raise your voice to our beloved daughter? ___

30. Are you to ever touch our beloved daughter before holy matrimony? ___

31. Are you familiar with pain? _____

32. Do you want to avoid pain? _____

33. Have you ever broken a bone? _____

34. Have you ever broken more than one bone? _____

35. Do you catch my drift? _____

36. Am I making myself clear? _____

37. Are you willing to face the possibility of immense pain and suffering for a single moment of temporary pleasure? ___

38. Do I need to show you my high-powered rifle collection? ___

LEGAL STATEMENT:

I, _____, being of sound mind and

body understand fully the responsibility I have to protect, respect, care

for, and protect (*I really like "protect"*) their beloved daughter,

<u>Tiffany Baker</u>. I am fully cognizant of the consequences

if I breech my contract of trust with Mr. ~~and Mrs.~~ _____ Baker

, and will most likely suffer great and intense personal pain and anguish

due to Mr. and Mrs._____ _____ Baker _____

enacting retribution upon my poor, wretched soul. I am to expect great

displeasure if their beloved daughter,_____ Tiffany Baker

, is in anyway harmed, disrespected, uncared for, or injured emotionally

or physically. I will not seek medical or personal damages if injured by

Mr. and Mrs._____ Baker _____ .

Name (printed):_____

Date: (day/month/year):_____

Social Security #: _____ - _____ - _____

Driver's License #: _____ State: _____

Signed in Blood:

.

_____

Use the sharp end of the attached needle to prick your finger:

──────────●

Passport Photo:

```
┌─────────────────────────────┐
│                             │
│                             │
│                             │
│   No glasses or sunglasses  │
│    Ears must be visible     │
│                             │
│                             │
│                             │
│                             │
└─────────────────────────────┘
```

Notary Public:

State of _____   *Affix Notary Stamp Here*

County of _____

This document has been subscribed and sworn before me this

_____

Day of _____, 20____ by

_____

Notary Public:

_____

My commission expires:

_____

Notary Signature:

_____

Made in the USA
Columbia, SC
22 April 2018